Mary Finch and the Grey Lady

S S Saywack was born in Guyana in 1955 and now lives in London, United Kingdom. He has published a number of books including the Mary Finch Mysteries, of which this book is the first, and has won a number of awards.

ALSO BY S S SAYWACK

Mary Finch and the Thief

Mary Finch and the Grey Lady

Mary Finch and the Spy

Mary Finch Endgame

Mary Finch Runaway, a prologue

***

Perdita, the Witch and the Toyshop

***

Inglestone Manor

Available as both eBooks and print books.

To contact the author: saywackwrites@gmail.com

or for more information visit: https:saywackwrites.com

Facebook page: https://www.facebook.com/SSSaywack/

S S SAYWACK

Mary Finch
and the
Grey Lady

A Mary Finch Mystery

Copyright © 2023 by Shiv Saywack

All rights reserved.

No part of this book may be reproduced in any form or by any electronic or mechanical means, including information storage and retrieval systems, without written permission from the author, except for the use of brief quotations in a book review.

First published 2021

 Created with Vellum

Where there is no imagination there is no horror.

Sir Arthur Conan Doyle

I

THE INCIDENT IN CHARING CROSS HOSPITAL

'No! No! No!' Mrs Grady cried.

The sudden outburst drew Mary Finch's attention and she hurried back to the breakfast room. The instant she entered, Mrs Grady flung down the newspaper she had been reading. She arose so quickly, her chair was knocked over and the cup of coffee she was drinking, she spilled. Her face went ashen as she stared dumbly into space.

'Ma'am, what's wrong?' Mary asked as she retrieved the chair, placing it back near her mistress again.

'Professor Cavendish?' Mrs Grady grimaced as if in pain, clutching the table so tightly that her knuckles whitened and the crockery rattled. 'Surely not he as well?'

'I'm sorry, ma'am—as well?' Mary asked. She reached out to steady the old lady, but Mrs Grady slumped heavily into her chair, taking several deep breaths and closing her eyes. When she opened them again, her hands came up to her mouth and she shuddered.

'No, this cannot be,' she said.

Before Mary could do or say anything, Mrs Grady was up. She charged out of the room, almost bowling Mary over. The maid's mouth gaped as she stared at the retreating figure of her mistress.

A few moments later, the Butler, Mr Venables, came rapidly into the breakfast room.

'A cab, Mary,' he said. 'Stop a hansom,' and pointed to the front door.

'A cab, Mr Venables?' Mary asked.

'Quickly, to take the mistress to Charing Cross Hospital,' the Butler said, pushing her out of the breakfast room and towards the door.

'Charing Cro… Mrs Grady… Is she ill…?'

The Butler's face reddened.

'Yes, Mr Venables,' Mary said and raced to do as she was asked.

The moment she flagged down an empty cab, the front door flew open and Mrs Grady rushed out. Her appearance startled Mary, she looked like a frightened animal that was being hunted.

In the next instant, the Butler bundled Mary some-what ungraciously into the cab alongside the old lady and thrust a newspaper into her hand, saying, 'The late news item. The Stop Press!'

Before Mary could ask what he meant, Mr Venables turned to the driver and ordered, 'Charing Cross Hospital. As quick as you can,' pressing some coins into his hand.

The driver clucked, 'Walk on, boy!' The whip cracked, the horse stumbled, and they were away.

Despite Mary's pleas and ignoring her concerns, Jane Rose Grady sat back in utter silence. Her cold eyes held a fixed indeterminate gaze, peering ahead into space but seeing nothing. She looked drained, old and worn; a woman of over sixty, as she was, and positively deathly. Her mouth was clenched, and a knot of hard muscle rippled her jaw.

A bare two months had passed since Mary become Mrs Grady's maid. In that time, she had never seen her mistress act in such a manner. The Irishwoman was usually cheer-ful, but of late, Mary sensed that the old lady was worried. Her bouts of melancholy were a source of whispered conversation in the household. Yet Mary had the impres-sion that whatever it was that troubled her, she quickly overcame it. However, the thought that she was putting on a brave face was always in the forefront of Mary's mind.

But today's outburst at breakfast was unheard of. That their destination was Charing Cross Hospital made Mary anxious about Mrs Grady's health, and she feared the worst.

'Can't your nag go any quicker?' Mary shouted to the driver. 'My mistress is ill!'

'He's doing his best,' the driver shouted back.

'He'll never win the Derby, will he?' Mary sneered. 'Come on, come on.' She rocked back and forth, urging the horse speedily onwards.

By now, they were trotting past the Royal Albert Hall towards Knightsbridge, heading in the direction of Wellington Arch. Much to Mary's distress, the traffic increased, slowing their progress. Cutting through Constitution Hill into the Green Park to the Mall was a thought, but the traffic there seemed to be moving even more slowly. Instead, they continued into Piccadilly. All the while, the horse snorted and puffed and kept up a dependable, uncomplaining pace, the rhythm of his drumming hooves steady.

At the top of Piccadilly, though, they were in the thick of it, and they were stopping and starting. Mary sat on the edge of her seat, willing the traffic out of the way, cursing each delay. She drummed her fingers nervously on the edge of the door and bit her lips frantically, wanting more speed. And all the time, to her consternation, Mrs Grady sat unmoving.

Finally, the cab turned into Charing Cross Road and Agar Street and arrived at the front steps of the hospital.

Mary asked, 'Shall I fetch a doctor?'

To her surprise, Mrs Grady rushed past her and descended on the receptionist like a demon. Her angry manner flustered the startled young man behind the desk, who stuttered and mumbled some words. Before he could finish speaking, Mrs Grady was rushing along the corridor and up the stairs, ignoring his protests.

Mary followed her mistress as well as she could while muttering apologies as they went. On several occasions, the old lady almost bumped into a nurse, or a doctor, or a patient, or a visitor. She disregarded their complaints and pushed past them dismissively.

Their destination was a room on the top floor. Just as they reached it, the door flew open. A lady in a grey dress, her face covered by a veil, dashed out. For a brief moment, she and Mrs Grady looked at each other, then the old lady shied back against the wall nervously. If it were possible for Mrs Grady's face to whiten further, Mary would swear that it did then.

Before she could ask what was the matter, there came a dreadful cry, like that of a wild animal, from the room. As if chased by the screams, the veiled lady ran quickly past them.

Mrs Grady rushed into the room and immediately shuffled back in shock. Mary grasped her shoulders when she saw the reason. In the bed by the window was a living nightmare. The old lady shook violently; her eyes flicked to the open door through which the woman left, and then back to the bed.

An old man, in his late sixties and as thin as a rake, lay in shredded nightclothes and drenched in sweat. He was fighting two orderlies who held his arms, and even with two nurses holding his legs, they battled desperately with him, such was his strength. His face hideously contorted, eyes wild and saliva foaming at his mouth, he was like a demon; an apparition from a ghastly nightmare with wailing screams and clawing fingers; a livid ghost from one of the Penny Dreadfuls Mary was so fond of reading.

When his eyes fell on to Mrs Grady, the old man stopped struggling. His mouth opened and contorted, screwing up tightly when a violent tremor shook him. It ran from his calves up to his thighs and into his stomach, then across his chest and finally to his head. He squirmed as if trying to escape those restraining him—as if trying to escape Mrs Grady—and released a hideous cry.

'Nefrusheri! Forgive me!'

In one supreme effort, he flung those who held him away, pushed out of his bed and ran towards the window. With a savage yell, he threw himself at the glass and he began to claw his way out as it shattered, oblivious to the shards slashing his arms and body, the blood flowing freely from his cuts. His head snapped back, his fright-ened eyes again falling on Mrs Grady.

'Spare me! I did not know!' he whispered to her in terror.

Turning, he placed his hand on either side of the window frame, preparing to leap when suddenly he became very still. His body relaxed and his arms fell to his sides and the blood dripped down his fingers to the floor. He exhaled heavily and began to sway. As if unable to support his weight any longer, his legs gave way and he collapsed on to the floor.

At the same moment, Mrs Grady fainted.

Mary quickly grasped and held the limp body of her mistress, supporting her as she toppled, controlling the fall so that the old lady's head rested against her lap. Only then did she look up.

Everyone was standing quiet and still, their unbelieving eyes fixed on the bloodied body of the elderly man on the floor. His face hideously contorted in the rictus of a silent scream, he lay dead where he had fallen.

THE STOP PRESS!

MRS GRADY AWOKE WITH A START. A nurse was wafting a phial of smelling salts under her nose and she shied away from the pungent odour as her eyes opened.

'You gave me a fright,' Mary said in relief.

She knelt beside Mrs Grady, who had been carried to a comfortable chair in an adjacent room, and held her hands, which felt cold and trembled. The old woman could hardly speak, but garbled something. Mary wondered if she'd said 'The woman in grey,' but she could not be sure. She saw the old lady's eyes flick nervously to the door, as if expecting to see something, perhaps the woman she spoke of. Perhaps it was the vision of the old man that filled her sight.

A doctor came and felt Mrs Grady's pulse.

'Fast!' he muttered.

'Is she all right?' Mary asked.

'Come, child, you're getting in the way. Wait outside,' he said pompously as he felt Mrs Grady's forehead.

'Yeah, but is she all right?'

'I said, wait outside.' His eyes gave the nurse an order and Mary found herself being pulled away and out of the room despite her complaints.

Once in the corridor, Mary peeped inside the room where the old man lay, which smelled both strongly of carbolic and pleasantly of violets. The man, who Mary assumed to be Professor Cavendish, rested where he'd fallen, his body frozen in a gruesome contortion as if rigor mortis had set in. But Mary knew from her talks with Dr Watson and Mr Holmes that such a condition came about hours after death, not minutes.

A nurse, covering Professor Cavendish with a sheet, look shocked. Almost as soon as the sheet touched the corpse, his blood seeped into the pristine white linen and blossomed like hideous red flowers.

Mary stopped the doctor who had just tended Mrs Grady.

'What happened?' she asked.

The doctor shook his head.

'I wish I knew,' he said. 'Is his daughter still here?' he asked the nurse.

'A lady in a grey dress?' Mary asked, and the doctor nodded. 'No. She left in a hurry, looked like she was frightened—can't say I blame her, seeing her dad like that.'

'That lady you came with, Nefrusheri, is she his wife?'

'Nefrusheri? No, she's Mrs Rose Grady, she ain't married to no one.'

'Grady? Mrs Grady?' The doctor lifted his head to the ceiling as if trying to remember something. His jaws jutted out. 'Ah! My mistake. Now I recall. His sponsor.'

'Sir?'

'Nurse, find some porters to take the body to the mortuary and start tidying up this room, for goodness' sake,' he said. 'The window will have to be repaired before it can be reoccupied. Speak to the premises manager about it.' He waved her away with several flicks of his hand.

'Sir,' Mary said again. 'Sponsor of what?'

'Oh! Some Egyptian Nile-type expedition thing,' he said busily, waving his hand once more. 'Finding tombs and long-lost Pharaohs. Digging things up. Mrs Grady. Yes, I read it in the *Times*. She financed it.'

They walked back into the other room. The old lady was still resting in the chair. Some colour had returned to her face.

'So, how's my patient? Still feeling a bit woozy? Mrs Grady, isn't it?' He took her pulse and nodded once more. 'Better. Much better.' He stood and placed a hand across her forehead. 'Still warm. Nurse, find out if the gentleman's daughter is still on the premises. If not, ask the administrator to see me. Well, Mrs Grady,' he turned his attention back to her, 'you seem better. It was a shocking sight to witness. I would recommend a day in bed once you're home, and Mother's cure-all—hot sweet tea— gallons of the stuff. Nurse, inform Dr Shepherd I'll perform the autopsy if he can assist me—though I suspect the cause will be heart failure.' Turning to Mary he said, 'Make sure your mistress does nothing taxing until tomorrow. As for you, Mrs Grady, take some time here to recover before going home.'

With that, he left.

Mary gave the old woman a curious look. Her eyes were closed as if she was deep in thought, but she was not asleep. It was then Mary remembered the newspaper given to her by Mr Venables. She was still carrying it.

There was only one item of late news to be found in the stop press:

Professor Hubert Cavendish, recently returned from Egypt, fell suddenly ill this last evening. He was taken to Charing Cross Hospital where his condition is described as critical.

'Critical?' Mary mumbled to herself as she gazed through the open door to the corridor where two porters were running past, pushing a trolley.

❈ 3 ❈

A MEETING IN THE KITCHEN

THEY WENT HOME in much the same silent way as they'd came, with Mrs Grady unwilling to speak. Her blank, unresponsive eyes steadfastly refused to acknowledge her maid and she wouldn't be dragged away from her inner thoughts, despite Mary's pleas.

Once they arrived at the Rose Garden, Mrs Grady's house in Holland Park, Mary led the old lady to her room. That her mistress did not complain and allowed herself to be helped to bed, almost as if she were an infant, worried Mary—she knew how independent her mistress was, and this was very out of character. It was obvious that her mind was still in Professor Cavendish's room at the Charing Cross Hospital.

Afterwards, Mary, standing absent-mindedly in the upstairs living room, at a loss for what to do, noticed

Ella, Mrs Grady's young ward, peeping round the door. The small girl looked frightened.

'Mary, is Mrs Grady all right?' Ella asked quietly and nervously, as if afraid of the answer.

'She'll be fine…' Mary glanced at the clock on the mantelpiece. 'Ella Sutton, shouldn't you be in school? It's nearly midday—you telling me you missed the whole morning?'

She grasped the girl's wrist, ignoring the protests, and walked her down the stairs.

'Fortune! Fortune!' Mary shouted. A ten-year-old girl from the West Indies, a maid the same age as Ella, appeared. 'There you are. Good girl. Take Miss Ella across to the school, Fortune.'

'B-b-but Mary,' Ella complained, 'I want to stay with Mrs Grady.'

'No buts. Tell Mrs Pyms whatever you want as to why you missed the morning, but not anything about Mrs Grady.' Mary wagged a finger in front of Ella's eyes. 'Is that clear? Not a word. And Fortune, I'll check your homework later.'

Fortune frowned.

'And less of the face, miss,' Mary huffed. 'You'll be grateful for Mrs Grady's charity one of these days. What other employer would care enough to send you to school and still pay you a wage? Go on, off with you both.'

With that, Mary started to dust. But before long,

unable to concentrate on such a simple task, she went to the kitchen.

It was an odd sight to see Mr Venables with his coat off. Even more so with his sleeves rolled up and seated at the table, diligently polishing the silver—one of her jobs. Wearing white Egyptian cotton gloves, he meticulously went about the task, his quiet grey eyes fixed on the spoon he held, his white hair combed neatly. He exuded an aura of authority with his perfectly straight back.

Cook placed a cup of tea before him. They both looked up and fell silent seeing Mary in the kitchen.

'Well?' Mary said. 'Let's have it.'

The Grady household was as far removed as it could possibly be from her last place of employment. There, such a demand would have not only been unheard of, but met with a severe reprimand from Mr Boots, the Butler. Here, Mr Venables and Cook had known Mrs Grady since childhood. They accompanied her from their homes in Ireland when she settled in London some thirty-odd years ago, so theirs was a long and deep friendship, and as such made it a pleasant house to work in. Mrs Grady demanded professionalism only with visitors. Mary easily fell into their informal ways and quickly became accepted as one of them. However, if they were going to tell her anything, Mary knew, she would have to work for it.

'Mind your own business, Mary Finch,' Cook said with a pleasant smile.

'This is my business. Remember I was there. Now, what's going on?'

'I recall a time when young girls like her knew their place,' Cook said to the Butler. Mr Venables, though, remained quiet, concentrating on his work.

'And a cup of tea would go down nice while you tell me,' Mary said, smiling.

'The gall of the girl,' Cook said. 'I think you know where the kettle is by now, Mary Finch.'

'Come on, you two. I've just seen something horrible, and I'd like to know what you know about it,' she pleaded. 'And don't tell me you don't know anything—you're thick as thieves and that's for sure.'

'It is a private matter of the mistress's,' Mr Venables said solemnly.

'Not so private that you two can't gab about it.'

'Private, nevertheless.'

'Do you know what I've just seen? I mean, I could tell you if I could describe it. That Professor Cavendish was off his mind. He even tried to jump out of a window. It took four people to hold him down, and he was thin as a stick and older than Mrs Grady. He was a demon. And the look on the mistress's face after... Blimey, the look on *his* face!'

'Private, nevertheless,' Mr Venables reiterated as he concentrated on polishing the silver.

Mary took a deep breath and was about to complain, when the door behind her opened. To everyone's surprise,

Mrs Grady stood in the doorway dressed in a nightgown. She pulled it tightly around her as if she was cold. Her skin was grey and her hair unkempt; her eyes still looked haunted.

'Tell her, Eileen,' Mrs Grady said loudly. Even so, her voice cracked.

'Rosie!' Cook almost dropped the bowl she was stirring.

'Rose?' Mr Venables stood up quickly, scattering the silver across the table.

'Tell her,' Mrs Grady said again, more softly. She edged up to the kitchen table, looking frail and every bit as old as she was, and drew out a chair. Slowly she eased herself down; the effort to get to the kitchen appeared to have tired her.

'Rosie, you can't be down here in the kitchen… dressed like that… You should be in bed…' Cook blustered. 'I mean, it's not done… what'll people think… no, no, no, you go back to bed this minute, and I'll make you a fine cup of tea… Mary, help the mistress up to her bedroom… come on, girl, make yourself useful…'

'Eileen O'Halloran, are you trying to tell me what I can and can't do in my own house?' Mrs Grady furrowed her brow as she spoke and sat back in her chair, a statement of intent: she would not leave.

'But you're not dressed! Goodness me, what'd people say if they saw you half dressed like that in my kitchen at this hour of the day?'

'It is *my* kitchen, I'll care to remind you, my dear,' Mrs Grady said. 'And quite frankly, if I parade around *my* kitchen in *my* birthday suit, at whatever hour of the day *I* choose, it is still *my* kitchen and *my* business if *I* do so.'

The smile that almost curled Mr Venables's lips fled under Cook's acidic glare.

'Now stop fussing like an old woman and get me a cup of tea. A doctor has prescribed it. Hot and sweet, he said. And one for Mary as well. She experienced the same shock as I.'

'I *am* an old woman, and I have *never* fussed in my life,' Cook said and placed the bowl down with a clatter. 'Well, it's a good thing we're not back in the old country, Jane Rose Grady. Just what would your mother have said if she saw you like this?' Cook pointed a wooden mixing spoon at her. 'That's what I'd like to know. And if she had ever seen you parading around in your birthday suit, she'd have taken a switch to your behind, for sure.'

'Hark!' Mrs Grady laughed and cupped her hands around her ears. 'Listen, my mother is speaking. What *is* she saying? Can anybody hear?'

Cook huffed as Mr Venables suppressed another laugh. 'Trust me, Rose Grady,' she said haughtily, 'the switch would have spoken volumes if I knew anything about that sainted woman. And it's brandy you need for shock, not tea. Any half-wit doctor should know that.'

'Tea, please, Eileen,' Mrs Grady said. 'And in a mug, if it's not too much trouble.'

Cook took the kettle away from Mary and dropped it with a clang on to the stove, muttering gruffly to herself in the process, while she emptied the teapot of the dregs and leaves. 'Birthday suit, my goodness! And in a mug, she says. What's the point of all that good china if it's to be in a mug?'

Mrs Grady pushed out one of the kitchen chairs with a foot, and indicated with her eyes for Mary to sit. The woman looked considerably aged. If Mary didn't know better, she would have said tormented. The anguish seemed to diminish her, to make her appear small and vulnerable. Even more so when she wrapped her arms around her shoulders and leant her elbows on to the table.

'I will tell you, Mary, if they won't,' she said, while looking down. 'I can't sleep anyway. I keep seeing Professor Cavendish each time I close my eyes. And in speaking of it, I might make some sense of it.'

❧ 4 ❧
THE CURSE OF THE
GREY LADY

IN THE QUIET of the kitchen, Mrs Grady began.

'Several years ago, Professor Cavendish, knowing of my interests in ancient Egypt and my association with organisations that promote women's suffrage, asked me to sponsor an expedition he had in mind. He was convinced that he knew the whereabouts of the tomb of an ancient Egyptian queen—Hatshepsut.'

Mrs Grady toyed with a fork as she spoke. She sat quietly for a minute, collecting her thoughts.

'Cavendish told me that Hatshepsut was the elder of the two daughters of Pharaoh Thutmose I. She married her half-brother, who became Pharaoh Thutmose II. On his death, the throne passed to an infant son born to one of his secondary wives—'

'Secondary wife?' Mary asked.

'It seems as if they had many wives alongside the one they first married.'

'Heathens!' Cook grumbled. 'One should have been enough for any man.'

'I dare say.' Mrs Grady smiled. 'Hatshepsut and Thutmose II's union produced a daughter, who, in that society, could not inherit the throne. As was customary, Hatshepsut became regent to the infant son, Thutmose III. That was in about 1479 BC.'

'Three and a half thousand years ago!' Mary marvelled.

'My interest was piqued. As Cavendish knew it would be. Hatshepsut was one of only a few women to hold such powers. In some three thousand years of Egyptian history, there would only ever be three.

'It may have been an attempt to preserve the throne for her stepson; maybe to reaffirm the legitimacy of her claims; or simply to forestall any controversies that made Hatshepsut reinvent herself. She ordered that she should be portrayed in hieroglyphs as a male pharaoh—bearded and muscled.'

The irony made the old lady laugh and Mary saw the youthful Mrs Grady surface from whatever depths she had been hiding.

'She was a successful pharaoh by all accounts. She was buried somewhere in the Valley of the Kings. Then she disappeared from history. Heaven's forbid! A successful woman!'

Again she laughed.

'Thutmose III, embarrassed by her success, had her virtually erased from the records. Her face was defaced and cut away from her statues and paintings. As a result, very little is known about her. Cavendish probably had the greatest knowledge of anyone about that queen.'

Cook poured tea into four enamel mugs while Mr Venables continued meticulously polishing the silver.

'So, I sponsored the expedition. That was a little over a year ago. Hatshepsut's tomb was never found. But Cavendish found another tomb—that of a high priestess to the queen. I have a photograph of those who found it, Mary. There was a plaque at the entrance of the tomb. I can't remember Cavendish's exact translation, but it read to the extent that whosoever is responsible for the violation of the tomb, death will follow them.'

'But ain't there a sign like that on all the tombs?' Mary said sarcastically. 'I mean, I read things like that in a Penny Dreadful. It's just there to frighten the grave robbers.'

Mary became aware of everyone's eyes, looking at her.

'H-hold on! Is any of you seriously telling me that Professor Cavendish died because of an ancient Egyptian curse?' Mary joked. 'I can tell you now,' she said more solemnly, 'no mummy killed him! I was there, remember?'

'Four members of the expedition have died since their

return from Egypt,' Mr Venables said gravely. 'Mr Sinclair, Bert Chambers and Selwin Barnet. And now Professor Cavendish. Each circumstance has been mysterious, to say the least. A fifth man died in Egypt.' Not once did his eye leave the fork he was buffing. 'The Grey Lady?' he asked.

Mrs Grady was silent. Her hands were cupped around her mug of tea as if warming herself. Mr Venables's eyes flicked up, and then down again.

'The Grey Lady,' Mr Venables continued. 'On the cartouche that contained the warning was the figure of a lady dressed in grey—Hatshepsut's high priestess. It was her tomb Cavendish found. There have been reports of a lady dressed in grey present at each of the deaths—'

'Wait a second—'

'One was seen exiting the train after Mr Sinclair's death. One spoke to Chambers in the church before he fell, and one was seen on the other side of the pond where Barnet drowned. She is always silent and wears a veil.'

'Now hold on!' Mary said firmly. 'All right, I grant some coincidence happens, and there was a lady in grey, with a veil at Charing Cross…' When she looked up, Mrs Grady was chewing her bottom lip; her eyes were vacant. 'But that was Mr Cavendish's daughter, not some avenging ghost. And she wasn't exactly happy at the prospect of seeing her old man dying, I could see that much.'

Mr Venables stopped polishing and was merely holding the fork between the folds of a soft cloth. He looked at Mrs Grady, who returned his gaze, and then at Mary.

'Daughter?' he asked.

'Yes.' Mary nodded. 'The doctor sent someone to find her.'

'Professor Cavendish's only daughter sailed with her husband for South Africa two weeks ago. I escorted her to the steamer at Southampton at Mrs Grady's request and saw her off personally.'

'But… then… who…?' Mary fell silent.

It was an unusual sensation, but the kitchen had become a strangely quiet place, and Mary was aware of the thrumming of her heart. She could picture the woman dressed in grey hastening away. The face, hidden under the veil, was odd. She'd thought it almost skeletal, but she put that down to her imagination, or a trick of the light or some such, and no more.

'It was foretold,' Mrs Grady whispered.

Cook huffed loudly and scraped her chair back, making a heavy screech against the flagstone floor. 'Stuff and nonsense,' she barked. 'A stupid ungodly thing to believe in if ever there was—'

'Cook!' Mr Venables shouted.

'Rosie!' Cook drew back in horror. 'God forgive me, Rosie. Please forgive me. It's just a stupid old woman talking who should know better. I would cut my tongue out before—'

'Sh-s-s,' Mrs Grady said softly and got up, went across and hugged her friend. 'I know, my dear. But there it is. I'll not apologise to anyone if I believe there is a chance. And I'm glad I know people like you not afraid to speak their minds.'

Mary looked at the two women in confusion.

'Tobias,' Mrs Grady said. 'On my dressing table is the photograph of the tomb opening ceremony. Please fetch it for me,' and the Butler quietly arose. He rolled down his sleeve, fixed his cufflinks, slipped into his jacket and adjusted the fall of the material. Only when he was properly dressed, did he leave.

'What do you mean foretold, Mrs Grady?' Mary asked. 'And a chance? For what?'

There was an emptiness that sometimes inhabited Mrs Grady's eyes that Mary noticed on occasion of late, especially when the old lady slipped deep into a state of melancholy. Now she saw it again, in that haunted stare.

'It has been over thirty years since I lost my husband,' Mrs Grady said. 'I still dream of him, Mary. I see Patrick on that fateful day, alone on the deck of his ship, the *Jane Rose*, as the icy waters engulf him. He sinks to the bottom of the ocean. He sees me and says not to worry because he is not dead, merely gone away, but he will always be there beside me.' Mrs Grady reached over and took Cook's hands and gave them a squeeze, and the two old ladies smiled at each other. 'And I believe he is. His presence is so powerful, I sometimes think I can see him with that cheeky smile on his lips and that wink of his eye that always made me laugh.'

'Aye.' Cook grinned quietly. 'He had that cocky way about him.'

'But what's this got to do with Professor Cavendish?' Mary asked.

'The greatest mystery of life is what happens after we die, is it not?' Mrs Grady said. 'Tell me, do you know what a medium is?'

Mary nodded. 'Someone who speaks to the dead, ain't it?'

'Eileen thinks I waste my time.' Cook was about to say something, but Mrs Grady placed a finger against her lips. 'Over the years, I have employed many mediums. Most were cheats and fakes. Most played parlour games to convince me that it was the spirit of Patrick Grady tapping or wailing or moving this and that about. Mr Venables is a difficult man to fool and easily saw through their tricks—unlike me.'

She smiled shyly. 'Call it foolish if you like, Mary. But I have heard of successes in America and France, even in Britain. The Queen, Mrs Lincoln and other eminent figures have sought the help of mediums. Some four months ago, I employed a girl to perform a séance. She was fourteen, not much older than you. Her recommendations were impeccable. Such a strange girl, I have never seen the like before. She had an odd presence, and it was an odd evening, none of which I can explain.'

Mrs Grady drew back and closed her eyes as if she was searching her memory. Then she continued in a quiet fashion, as before.

'The aura that surrounded her grew as the evening progressed. It-it… frightened me. She said she could feel the spirit of Patrick nearby, but she could not reach him. Something stood in her way. Even so, I thought I saw Patrick—oh! It was he, I was sure, in that damned velvet jacket he knew I hated and he loved to wear. Then she fell into a deep trance. I was assured it was normal, that she was becoming one with the spirits, to be used as a gateway between the here and the hereafter. But when she spoke with a voice that was not her own…' Mrs Grady shivered. 'It was a dreadful sound that haunts me still.'

'It was the Devil,' Cook said softly, and she looked away.

'It may well have been for all that has happened since,' Mrs Grady continued. 'I was ready to listen for my Patrick's voice. Instead, I heard another. It was a fearful voice, like that of an animal, something primae-val, old and wretched. Some malevolence had taken over her. Her mother tried to wake her, but could not. Then the voice warned me that I was trespassing.'

Cook crossed herself; she mumbled some quiet words of prayer.

'I shall never forget that demon's words,' Mrs Grady said. ' "*I have slept for three thousand years, why dost thou disturb me? I am the keeper of the night. I am the Grey Lady. My breath is death. My curse is upon you and those that would dare wake me from my sleep.*"

'Her mother said that once in a trance, her daughter is at the beck and call of any spirit strong enough to bridge the gap between worlds. When the demon released her, there was such fear in the child's eyes, such terror, it was all she could do to collect her belongings before fleeing my house. They did not even wait to collect their fee. Ever since, they have been deaf to my queries, and in no uncertain terms, have indicated their wish to have nothing more to do with me.'

'Money is always the driving force of such confidence tricksters.' Mr Venables, who had returned, was listening quietly. 'Yet theses two refused payment the several times I went to see them. Even though I insisted, they would not let me in to discuss the matter, nor accept a fee.'

'Before she left, the child warned me to desist with my endeavours or death would be my companion,' Mrs Grady said. 'But it was too late. By then, Professor Cavendish had already opened the tomb of Hatshepsut's priestess: she who was called Nefrusheri.'

Mary's mouth dropped open.

'That's the name the professor called you,' she said.

'Curious, isn't it?' Mrs Grady nodded and fell quiet.

'And he asked for your forgiveness,' Mary added, puzzled.

Do I believe in ghosts and spirits? Mary was not sure, she always thought herself rational. But she could not help recalling, when she'd lain ill in her friend's house, not two months ago, she thought she'd seen the ghost of Tom Norris keeping watch over her, and it was obvious that these three people believed in such things. A Grey Lady she had seen, and in Cavendish's eyes, she recognised the terror of his belief in the Egyptian priestess.

Mrs Grady took the photograph from Mr Venables and showed it to Mary. Five proud, smiling men, dressed formally in jackets, collars and ties, despite the undoubted heat they were in, looked back to a camera that recorded their image for all times. All five were now dead. A deeply carved and richly decorated sarcophagus was in front of them, the last resting place of the high priestess Nefrusheri, the Grey Lady.

'This is the day we awoke death,' Mrs Grady said.

A VISIT

THE NEXT DAY, Mrs Grady asked Mary to take a message to the medium who had performed the séance. Perhaps Mary would fare better than Mr Venables, who had tried several times to see her, but on each occasion had been refused an audience. Lorna Denbie and her mother resided in Soho, so it was an opportunity for Mary to visit her friend, Archie Dibble, who lived nearby in Baker Street.

It was a pleasant morning walk accompanied by Ella and Fortune, who, to their relief, did not have school today. The sun was warming, and after such a difficult winter, it was a moment to daydream and enjoy the first cherry blossoms of spring.

From her mountaintop redoubt, the vast expanse of the Sahara spread out before her like an arid ochre carpet as far as the eye could see... Mary's thoughts trav-

elled far in her reverie, the stories from her Penny Dreadfuls always in her mind. *Commissioned by the Royal
Archaeological Institute to find the famed City of Gold,
Lady Mary Finch stood on the threshold of glory. But she
was assailed on all sides by the lost tribes of the desert
that wanted the secret kept from prying eyes. She had
only five shells left in her pistol, and there seemed no
hope of rescue. She would have to rely on the Finch guile
if she was to survive...*

She took a diversion on her way to Baker Street, past
the residence of the Grimwigs, her last employers, where
she had been the scullery maid. Just how awful that
winter was, came back to her and spread itself out inside
her mind.

The house was abandoned, she noticed, locked up,
awaiting new owners. It looked forlorn and lonely and
not the imposing residence that she remembered it once
to have been. She glanced up to the window of her old
attic room and gave a rueful grin. It lost its charm that
day, barely two months ago, when she was accused of
theft, and now it was just a house with bad memories.

In proving her innocence against the false accusations, she'd come close to being murdered. The faces of
those who died, especially Tom Norris, haunted her. She
could quite easily understand Mrs Grady's visions of her
long-dead husband. After all, she often saw Tom in her
dreams and could taste the acrid water of the Thames that
so nearly claimed her life.

Her old employer numbered blackmail amongst his professional skills. He used her. But her success was his downfall. Even so, the law was yet to catch up with him. Her anger at him and his awful family, however, was tempered when she was hired by Mrs Rose Grady. That was the best thing that could have happened to her.

Soon they entered Baker Street. When they passed number 221, Mary stopped and gazed up at the windows of flat B. There was no sign of life. She could not hear the sound of the violin. Either Mr Sherlock Holmes was out on a case or still asleep. Or perhaps he and Dr Watson were deep in conversation, busy calculating a theory to solve some baffling crime.

What would Mr Holmes make of Egyptian curses, strange demises, mediums and séances, and an even stranger grey lady that Mrs Grady believed to be an Angel of Death? Surely there existed things that even his clinical mind could not explain?

She walked on.

Ahead was Archimedes Dibble's pie shop. Without a shadow of a doubt, the best pie shop in London—although Mary could be biased. A kinder set of people she did not know; the Dibbles were her oldest friends. In her desperate hour of need, they welcomed her with no questions asked.

Even before she reached the shop, Dorothy Dibble (who everyone called Dot) and her younger sister, Sally (who everyone called Sossie), rushed out, and in their excitement almost collided with Ella and Fortune. An explosion of noise shook the street as the four girls began to shout and play chase along the pavement.

'Watch for the traffic,' Archie Dibble, a well-built boy of sixteen, bellowed.

Sossie, the youngest of the four, stopped, turned, and gave an elegant curtsy to her big brother. Archie returned a pleasant half bow. Sossie then placed her thumbs in each ear, wiggled her fingers and stuck her tongue out, while the others giggled loudly and ran off.

While Grandpa Dibble prepared the shop and his wife finished off the baking, Mary and Archie sat and talked. She valued his take on Mrs Grady's story. Much of what happened, she said, occurred before she joined the household, but she told him what she saw at the hospital and what Mrs Grady said in the kitchen.

'Clairvoyants?' Archie mocked. 'Things that go bump? She's been taken in. Don't she know that? I mean, that's what these people do, con you out of your money by promising to find your dear dead dad or mum, or uncle Dick or aunt Bess, just so you can have a word with them about how well they're doing in heaven.'

'Mrs Grady believes her, Archie—'

'More money than sense—'

'But the medium's not taken a penny from her,' Mary said. 'Not even a fee for the time she was there last. In fact, Mr Venables says she doesn't want anything to do with the mistress.'

Archie gave her a look of disbelief.

'If conning money were their motive,' Mary said, 'then Mrs Grady would be the one they'd choose to con, surely? She's bloomin' rich. But the things that have happened—I can't explain them.'

'The woman, you mean? The one you saw? Plenty of women have grey dresses. Even Grandma has one.'

'But to see one then—'

'You know what I mean. It's ghost stories like those in the books you're so fond of reading.' Archie laughed, shook his head and muttered disparagingly, 'And why grey? Why not black? Black's more scary, ain't it? I mean, I'd rather have a woman in black haunting me than one in grey,' he joked. 'Egyptian curses! There's a trick involved. There always is. She's being conned!'

Mary did not know what to think. The only thing she was sure about was that Mrs Grady believed. That was why Mary was asked to see the medium, to persuader her to agree to another séance and to return her uncollected fee.

'Look, Archie, Mrs Grady's not one to make things up; she's pretty right up here,' and Mary tapped her head, while Archie gave her a sceptical look. 'She said she even saw her late husband when they had that last séance. I think she's worried. The curse says death would follow her, and it has—so who wouldn't be worried? I mean, five people have died in mysterious ways, and that's no trick.'

'Well, about those deaths. Look, I get the Grey Lady thing, but who's to say it's not just a coincidence?'

She'd considered the possibility. But for a lady dressed in grey to be there on each occasion—that was odd to say the least.

'Five people from the same expedition?' Mary said and shook her head. 'All dying within months of each other? You see what's strange, Archie, is that the medium predicted this before Mrs Grady even knew they had opened the tomb, let alone found a curse or seen a drawing of a lady in grey. All that was happening in Egypt, three thousand miles away, when Mrs Grady was holding her séance. If it was a con, how could they have known any of these things before they happened? If Professor Cavendish didn't find a tomb, then the medium would look a blinkin' fool with her predictions, wouldn't she? For all anyone could know, the drawing could have been of a lady in a blue dress or a red one, or even of a crab. It's a bloody good guess, if that's what it was.'

Archie screwed up his face and mumbled, 'I mean, do you believe in all that? You know, ghost things?'

Mary was quiet. She looked around. It was in this very room she saw, or thought she saw, Tom Norris's ghost sitting beside her when she was on death's door. No one else saw him as he waited patiently, keeping sentry duty until she recovered. Was he real? Or did her imagination conjure him when she was ill, and had he been the product of a fever and no more?

'I don't know,' Mary said eventually. 'But Archie, don't you never wish you could speak to your mum and dad? I do sometimes.'

Like Archie, she too was an orphan. Her question, however, made him uncomfortable. The boy's unconvincing shrug of defiance was not lost on her—he missed them as much as she missed her parents, but he never talked about them.

'All I've got is one photograph of them,' Mary said. 'I can't even remember their voices, though that aunt who looked after me said Mum's was a beautiful soprano in the church choir. At least you knew your mum and dad.'

Mary shook her head, the memory always made her sad. Remembering her task for Mrs Grady, she pushed the thoughts aside before she succumbed to self-pity.

'Come with me, won't you, Archie? I could use some company.'

'What am I going to do there, Mary? You'll only get annoyed if I say something stupid, like *what's all this lark about, then?* And that won't help you persuade her to go back to Mrs Grady.'

'But you won't say that,' she said.

'I might. And if she starts all the mediuming stuff, I might even giggle.'

'No, you won't, it's not like you.'

The quickness of her words and the pleading look she tried to hide made Archie fall back on the bed, laughing.

'Are you scared, Finchie? Is that what *this lark* is all about?'

Mary folded her arms and pouted. She glared daggers at him, causing him to laugh more.

'Well?' he sniggered.

'It's nothing to do with being scared,' she said haughtily. 'It's just I ain't never been to a clairvoyant's house before.'

'Oh! And I have, I suppose?'

'Come on, Archie.' She grabbed his arm and gave it a tug to get him to rise from the bed. 'It's only in Berwick Street, just down the road a bit.'

'We-ellll, I might come,' Archie mused, eying the ceiling in an absentminded way and pursing his lips. 'I can do some shopping for Grandma in the market. Oh! But it's soooo far, and then there's Dot and Sossie to look after. Ella and Fortune, since they're here too… and today can be busy with all the customers… and Grandpa's getting on… and Grandma…'

Mary scowled and thumped Archie on the arm as he fell back once again, giggling.

'Berwick Street, you say?' Archie shivered in mock fright. 'Scary ghosts… O-ooo!'

Mary gave him a broad smile as he got up to go with her.

'You know what I don't get, Archie?' She slipped on her coat. 'It's why the spirit of Nefrusheri spoke English. I mean, shouldn't she be speaking Egyptian?'

❧ 6 ☙

THE CLAIRVOYANT

TWENTY-TWO BERWICK STREET fronted on to a road of stalls and benches, barrows and carts, and was noisy and busy at that hour. It was a shabby grey-black building in a street of other shabby grey-black buildings with dark windows that frowned at each other from across the street.

Mary and Archie squeezed past shoppers and traders to stand in front of a door with peeling black paint. Pinned to it was a weathered handwritten card that said it was the residence of Mrs Denbie and her daughter, the clairvoyant.

Mary gave a quiet, nervous knock. A surly sallow-faced maid answered. She kept them waiting several minutes, and afterwards, they were taken up a flight of stairs to the first floor and shown into a pleasant living room furnished with sofas, chairs and dark tables and cabinets. The stuffy odour of incense hung heavily in the air. The curtains were half drawn and the room was mostly in shadows. Opposite, where they'd entered, a half-open door led to another room, behind which someone's violent coughs and gasping wheezes punctuated the silence every so often.

Mary glanced around nervously. The walls were decorated with posters in frames and the occasional play-bills, marking the Denbies out as theatre people. One poster showed Mrs Denbie as a member of the *Four Fabulous Musketeers,* a quick-change comedy troupe, fresh from engagements in Washington, Boston and New York, now playing the theatres of London. It was several years old.

The most recent poster was of a Madame Zanaib and her daughter, Veda. *With a direct link to the spiritual plane and the supernatural regions beyond, the all-seeing oracle knows all, sees all and tells all,* it announced. The oracle held consultations, every Monday afternoon at the behest of a wealthy benefactor, a prominent woman of society, in rooms in Soho. From between the printed words, the faces of Mrs Denbie and her pale daughter stared back in sober earnestness.

Mary fidgeted anxiously after the maid left. In front of her, illuminated by a thin shaft of light from the window, sat Mrs Denbie, as if caught by a beam of a spotlight. A slim, elegant woman in her early forties, she was seated on a sofa and motes of dust danced around her. Her jet-black hair shone brightly and was set in a tight bun. Her dark eyes were a vivid contrast to her pale, expressive round face. She wore a plain black dress.

She indicated with a graceful wave of her arm for them to sit opposite.

Beside her sat the living ghost who was her daughter. Lorna Denbie was as tall as her mother, but thin and gaunt. Her deeply sunken cheeks defined the structure of her face, and long black lashes enclosed dark round eyes. Her lips were red rubies. If it were possible, her hair seemed blacker than that of the woman who sat beside her, and if that was not striking enough, her complexion was almost pure alabaster. She sat bolt upright, like a shop mannequin with a perfectly straight back, robed in black, an unmoving spectre at the end of the Chesterfield sofa.

The apprehension instilled by the wraith-like figure made Mary stutter the reason for her visit. She did her best to plead Mrs Grady's cause, even handing over the uncollected fee due to Lorna from her visit to Holland Park. But neither woman would take it and Mary placed it anxiously on a table beside them, apologising for doing so with a forced smile. A heavy, nervous silence greeted her when she'd finished.

There was something strained in the air. In the uncomfortable wait, Mary was aware of Lorna's roaming gaze. It flicked between her and Archie, an unrelenting examination. Mary fidgeted with the locket she wore while Archie scanned the room, his eyes unable to settle on any object long enough to hold his attention. But neither dared look directly at the ghost that was Lorna Denbie.

Noises from the street drifted in through the window: the shouts of hawkers, horses neighing, the clip-clopping of their hooves, the crunching of wheels on stone. Someone was laughing, somewhere a baby cried, people argued, all bracketed by the hacking coughs from behind the half-open door that only served to make the Denbies' silence even more oppressive. Above all of this, Mary could hear the frantic beating of her heart.

Mrs Denbie roused herself. It was as if she had been in a daydream and now was back in the present again.

'Your mistress asks much.' She hesitated, as if choosing her words carefully. 'A great evil surrounds her. We would not have taken the commission in the first place had we known what would be released. Something base crossed over from the nether world that day. It is a wickedness that will not be sated until it has completed its unholy purpose. It seeks your mistress's destruction and an end to those who wronged it. Even now, it gorges on its hatred.'

'But Mrs Denbie, surely you can help her,' Mary pleaded. 'I mean, already five people have died—'

'We have read about Professor Cavendish.' Mrs Denbie's eyes fell on to the newspaper on a low table —

The Unfortunate Death of Eminent Egyptian Explorer, the headline announced.

'I mean, isn't there some potion or thing you can give her to protect her?'

'It is not as simple as that. Rabbit's feet and four-leaf clovers will not dissuade the demon. It needs to be returned from where it came, and that is an endeavour fraught with danger.'

'How returned? Some sort of exorcism?'

Mrs Denbie nodded.

'You can do it, can't you?'

'Not I, but Lorna can.' She reached across and placed her hand over her daughter's. 'But it would put her in great peril, and I am reluctant to expose her to such jeopardy.'

'Mama, surely we can help?' Lorna said.

Mary was startled. Lorna Denbie's voice was high and thin; the cadence suggested someone of a much younger age. Even as she spoke, her eyes never left Mary.

'It was I who released that thing,' Lorna said.

Mrs Denbie shook her head and turned her attention fully to her daughter. 'No. I forbid it. Such spirits are not easily pacified. I will not have you placed in danger. The demon will do its work, and when that is completed it will return of its own volition from where it came.'

'But Mama, how can I have this?' Lorna complained churlishly. 'Its work will only be completed on the death of Mrs Grady. It was my fault it came. I allowed it to pass. These deaths are on my hands.'

'We have spoken of this already,' Mrs Denbie said. 'At our first meeting with Mrs Grady, your warning was clear. Mrs Grady chose to ignore it. The fault is hers and hers alone. She must bear the consequences. We will not speak of it again.'

'It passed by my grace, Mama,' Lorna said with a pout.

'You were only a doorway.' Mrs Denbie's voice was raised. 'It was she that wanted it open.'

'But Mrs Denbie, please,' Mary said. 'Mrs Grady didn't know what was happening in Egypt at that time. She couldn't have stopped them doing what they did because it was too late by then. Surely you can do something?'

'I fear for my daughter's soul,' Mrs Denbie said. 'I do not want the vengeance of this demon to fall on her and she to be lost in the half-world between existence from where it came.'

Lorna turned to her mother, a defiant look on her face.

'But I am much stronger than before, Mama.'

'I forbid it!' Mrs Denbie snapped. She turned abruptly and presented a stark face towards Mary. 'Our audience is over. Convey our regrets to your mistress. I would ask her to refrain from contacting us again. She has paid us our fee; there is no more to discuss.

There is nothing more we can do for her in this matter.'

From the hidden room, the spluttering coughs, interspersed with the name, Frances, grew louder and more insistent.

'Father!' Mrs Denbie whispered and hurried over to the voice.

When she left, the room once again descended into an oppressive silence. Outside, the clouds passing over the sun caused the light filtering through the half-drawn curtain to rise and fall. When Lorna Denbie did not speak, Mary arose hesitantly. She looked over to Archie for help, but the boy shrugged his shoulders.

Mary's head drooped in frustration. Like Mr Venables, she too had failed. Mrs Grady would be disappointed. She mumbled a thank you and was about to leave when she felt a finger brush her shoulder. Lorna Denbie had risen, quiet as a ghost, to stand beside her.

'I will speak further to Mama,' she whispered. 'I'm sure I can persuade her otherwise. Tell Mrs Grady that all is not lost.'

Mary returned a kindly smile and pleaded, 'At least tell me how she can protect herself or kill it. All we know is that the ghost or spirit, or whatever it is, is a woman and she dresses in grey.'

Lorna maintained her steady gaze and said, 'It is the form the demon takes to exact its retribution, that of a woman dressed in grey. After each occasion, it becomes an amorphous spirit that cannot be harmed or killed: it can only be sent away, back to where it came.' She thought for a second. 'Not five years ago, London was plagued by just such a malevolent demon that killed many women until it too was sent away.'

Mary heard Archie mumble a name and her brow furrowed. She stuttered, unable to get her words out, and took a deep breath.

'Jack? The Ripper, you mean… Jack?' she whispered.

Lorna Denbie said nothing. She stood, silent and rigid like a statue. Mary's mouth fell open.

'Was it *you* that sent him away?'

Lorna shook her head.

'But you know who did? You do, don't you?' Mary asked desperately and reached out her hand towards Lorna. The girl shrank back in alarm. 'Tell me who that was. If you can't help us, maybe that medium can.'

'I cannot,' Lorna said.

'But why? Look, Miss Denbie. I mean, if it's money, I'm sure my mistress will pay what you ask—for him or you—'

'It is not money. It is just… I cannot tell.' Something was clearly troubling her. She seemed afraid, as if she had spoken a secret and was frightened of being found out. Her voice became urgent. 'I am sorry. You must go. I will speak to Mama…'

'But—'

'I promise, I shall…'

For a second, she seemed confused, as if lost. She took a deep breath and became calm; she managed a weak smile, yet something seemed to pain her again.

'T-tell me, w-what is that?' Lorna asked. 'May I see it?'

She screwed her eyes up, a curious gaze, and was looking at the piece of jewellery Mary wore. The heart-shaped locket, which belonged to Mary's mother, had been snapped in half. It contained a photograph of her brother, Daniel.

Mary removed the chain from around her neck and placed it in Lorna's hand. The girl looked at it, turned it over and ran her finger across the photograph, and then against the sharp broken edge. In an instant, she flinched. It was as if a bolt of electricity had shocked her. A shudder ran up her body. She swayed and her eyes rolled and wandered aimlessly.

The next moment, Lorna Denbie gasped and dropped the locket.

Mary and Archie jumped in fright; blood was dripping from between Lorna Denbie's clenched fingers. She slowly opened her fist and gazed in disbelief. Her penetrating scream shook the room as she ran wildly towards her mother.

7

DANGER!

IN THE SMALL ROOM, the scream was like a gunshot. The reverberation rang in Mary's ears as she retrieved the locket from the floor and hurriedly followed Lorna Denbie. Once through the door, she and Archie stopped, rooted in shock.

The curtains were drawn, and a single oil lamp lit the room with a sickly yellow light. A musty, foetid odour of an unaired room, permeated the air. An old man, almost a ghost and as white as the nightshirt he wore, reclined in the bed. The very spectre of death, he glistened with sweat. The image of Professor Cavendish invaded Mary's mind. The spectre's eyes were half-closed, his cheeks sunken in his cadaveric face, and he held a towel with a trembling hand into which he coughed.

He wiped his mouth with the towel, and it was streaked with blood. Speckles of red dotted the front of his white nightshirt and the sheet around him. A bottle of laudanum was clutched in his hand. His bare arms were heavily tattooed with nautical references—ships and anchors and compasses that said he was once a sailor.

On a cabinet by the window were a small free-standing crucifix and a porcelain statue of a saint. The arrangement gave the impression of a shrine. Several framed photographs stood on the table of the old man when he was younger and they confirmed that he was indeed a seaman. A lone candle burned amongst them.

'What did you do to my daughter?' Mrs Denbie screamed. She held the sobbing, shaking girl tightly.

'Nothing, Mrs Denbie,' Mary said, horrified at the sight of Lorna's bloodied hand.

'What is it?' Mrs Denbie said to her daughter. 'Open your hand, let me see.' The sight of the bloody palm brought an angry flush to her face. 'Out! Get out!' she shouted at Mary and Archie. 'Get out!'

'No, Mama,' Lorna said, taking her mother's hand. 'No! I am all right, Mama. It was just... I did not expect it.'

'Expect it... what happened?'

Lorna's eyes widened as she fixed Mary with an intense stare.

'I was holding her locket—'

'You saw something?' Mrs Denbie said. 'Your gloves? Were you not wearing your gloves?'

'Mama...I... I–'

'You must wear your gloves. You know what happens when you don't. How often must I tell you?' Mrs Denbie's voice was almost hysterical.

'Frances!' the ghost in the bed shouted, and then coughed violently. His thin arm shot up and grasped Mrs Denbie's dress, pulling her towards him. 'The child made a mistake and no more,' he wheezed. 'Now, she saw something. Is that not so, Lorna?'

Lorna was quiet. Mrs Denbie gathered her nearer and dabbed a handkerchief against her daughter's palm. But when the blood was wiped away, the skin was unbroken.

Mary glanced nervously to Archie who, seeing the undamaged palm, stared at it as well.

'My… vision was… of her,' Lorna said hesitantly, looking at Mary through narrowed, nervous eyes. 'You are two people. You are incomplete. There is a part of you that is missing. It has been lost to you, and you seek it with fervent hope. I saw a child. I-I-I thought—'

'Danny?' Mary gasped.

'A young man. Yes, yes!' Lorna nodded, but to herself only. 'The chain that bound you together is broken. He is adrift. He is in great danger. He will be lost to you forever if he is not found soon. He so wishes to be found—'

'Danger?' Mary took a step forward, only for Mrs Denbie to raise her hand quickly, stopping her from coming nearer.

'I-I-I broke the connection too soon. Death surrounds

him. But no! I do not understand it. How is it that he is two people? How can that be so?' Lorna Denbie looked tired. She muttered quietly and indistinctly as if attempting to make sense of her vision.

'Please, tell me more,' Mary said. 'I've been looking for Danny for years. If you know where he is, please tell me. Look, I've got some money—here...' She frantically rummaged through her bag and brought out a few pounds. Some coins dropped onto the floor and Archie stooped to retrieve them. 'It's all I've got...but I can get more...'

Lorna shied away and shook her head.

'Frances!' the ghost in the bed shouted again. With some difficulty, he reached up to clutch Mrs Denbie's hand. His bony fingers gripped hers tightly, pulling her closer.

'Father, no!' Mrs Denbie said, comprehending his look.

'Yes!' he replied. 'You cannot protect her all her life. Lorna is strong. She is learning all the time and getting stronger each day. She must finish what was started. She must help Mrs Grady, and this poor girl.' His face winced in pain as a fit of coughing overtook him again.

There was fear in Mrs Denbie's eyes. Her face contorted with worry. She seemed to be fighting her own demons as she leant forward to comfort the old man. Soon his coughing abated, and as he lay back, only his wheezing disturbed the silence. Even the sounds from the street below his window were muted.

'My dear, Lorna must stand on her own two feet,' he spoke softly. Gathering his composure, he stifled the cough that rasped his throat. 'She has greatness within her.'

He was clearly proud as he reached out his hand for his granddaughter to take.

'Her destiny is to help others with her skills. She cannot pick and choose who they might be. She has inherited her grandmother's strength as well as her gifts. But in her, they are stronger. And her grandmother will protect her. That shield will keep her safe, no matter what demon assails her. She must help.'

Mrs Denbie shook her head. 'Must she help all and everyone who seeks her?' she whispered.

'She must help with this. What is the use of her gift if it is closeted?' He coughed loudly, unable to contain himself any longer, and she supported him and rub his back until the fit ended. 'If only I was not so weak,' he said to Lorna.

As the old man sat back, his chest rattled when he took deep breaths. He closed his eyes and his face was like a mask of death.

'I am not long for this world, Frances. Soon I shall be reunited with your mother. We will both be there for Lorna. We will protect her in ways that others cannot. But she must help. Give your permission, I beg.'

'But what if I lose her?' Mrs Denbie whispered hoarsely.

'My dear, you will never lose her. Do you not understand? Lorna will always be here with us, come what may. Look and behold the wonder of your daughter and what she is becoming. Her spirit is too great to be contained.' His sunken face glowed with pride.

Mrs Denbie went to the window to gaze out at the street below. She wrung her hands, and then wrapped her arms closely around her body, hugging herself, as if she was cold.

'Tomorrow is Wednesday,' Mrs Denbie mumbled, but did not turn to look at Mary. 'Tell your mistress to expect us at noon. Lorna must rest and prepare herself before then. But tell her…' and she gazed at her father, 'I allow this to happen unwillingly.'

The old man held out his hands to her, and as she took them, he whispered, 'It is the right thing, Frances.'

'You'll help me, too?' Mary held her breath, fearful Lorna would refuse. She reached out an arm towards the girl, then drew it back sharply, afraid to touch her.

'I will help,' Lorna said firmly. 'But I cannot today. When we meet again, I will see what I can do.'

She looked tired and weary, and in spite of Mary's insistence, Lorna Denbie could not be persuaded to add further to her vision of Daniel Finch.

Mrs Denbie demanded they leave; her father required

tending and her daughter needed rest. The maid escorted them to the door.

As they walked away, Mary turned back with a desperate glance. Mrs Denbie was watching them from the window of her father's bedroom. Anger clouded her face.

What had her daughter seen? Mary wondered. She had gone there on a mission for Mrs Grady and did not expected to find Danny waiting instead. Her brother was adrift, Lorna said. Daniel Finch was in danger, but he wished to be found.

8

MARY'S WORRIES

'Poor old bloke,' Archie said. 'Consumption, I reckon.'

Mary was quiet. Her head was down. She told herself she was rational. While Mrs Grady believed in such things as spirits, she wasn't sure how much she believed. But, she never met the Denbies before, yet Lorna knew about how she longed to be reunited with her brother. As Lorna held her locket, Daniel somehow reached out across the void to her.

'A month, maybe two I should think is all he's got,' Archie said. 'Not that I'm a doctor, mind.'

They pushed their way into Oxford Street, walking side-by-side, and diminished in size amongst the tall buildings that stood around them. Mary hardly noticed the swarm of people flitting butterfly-like, visiting one shop or the next, passing them by unnoticed. Her thoughts drifted back through time, leaving the present and Archie behind.

An aunt she barely remembered took her in after her parents died. Mary and Daniel were separated, and she had been given the locket as a keepsake, a reminder of her family and especially of him. She did not know where her aunt lived—she was too young to remember that sort of detail—only that it was on the other side of the river, somewhere in south London. Her memory was vague, but that much she knew.

'But he seemed in good spirits, didn't he?' Archie said. 'I mean, for someone who's dying.'

They crossed the street and she continued walking in silence.

'I took one of their playbills,' Archie said after a while. 'They had a stack of them, so I reckon they wouldn't miss one. Nice picture of her and her daughter, though she's a weird one. The daughter, I mean. That pale face. White, even. She could be a bleedin' ghost herself.'

Archie handed Mary the leaflet for Madame Zanaib and her daughter, Veda, who, every Monday, held private consultations in rooms in Soho. Mary took it mechanically, but her eyes were looking down at the pavement.

If she were to find her brother, she would need to find her aunt. Her aunt would know where he went, surely? How else could Mary find him? One thing she was certain, it was that aunt who took her to the house of her first employers, the Fortesques, and that was in Camden Town. And Camden Town would be the place to start her search.

But she remembered the Fortesques with horror. How the young master bullied her. How he poured dirty water on the floor, knowing she'd have to mop it up. She worried about seeing them again.

'Looks like they're doing a tour around England soon.' Archie looked over, but Mary's eyes were still on her feet as they marched along.

Archie nodded his head sagely. *'Yeah, Archie, I reckon they are.* Think they'll continue if her old man cops it? *Probably, Archie, after all, they're theatre people, and the show must go on, you know.* Yeah, I reckon you're right, professional to the end. And who knows? Maybe the old man will come back as a ghost when they're on stage. *What? Be part of the act, Archie?* Yeah, Mary, why not? *Yeah, Archie, he could be the visionary from the other side and tell her stuff and things.* Mary, do you think they'll have to change the playbill? *Why, Archie?* Well, to include him on it. *That's a thought, Archie.* But then again, Mary, it might be better if they didn't. *Why's that, Archie?* Well, won't it be difficult to explain?'

Mary stopped. Her brows knitted as she looked at him quizzically.

'What are you going on about?' she asked.

'Me? Oh, nothing,' Archie said with a smirk. 'That

was a good point you made about him helping them when he passes…' He laughed at Mary's puzzled face. 'Never mind. Care to enlighten me just what it is you're thinking? Because you ain't heard a word I've said.'

'I have to see the Fortesques,' Mary said.

'Mrs Fortesque? And her son, Noah? Why?'

'Because I need to ask her something.'

'So she can give you another bash around your head?' He huffed.

Mary rubbed the scar behind her ear with a rueful scowl, remembering how she got it. It was from a blow given to her by Mrs Fortesque, when she was employed as a maid—her first job. Not long after, she ran away—to remain would have been madness. That was when she first met the Dibbles.

Archie shook his head. 'It's about Danny, I'm thinking.'

'She won't know much about him, Archie. No, it's about that aunt of mine, who got me the job. I need to find her to find Danny, and for that, I'll have to see Mrs Fortesque. But I can't do that until I've finished running this errand for Mrs Grady.'

'You sure she was an aunt, the one who gave you the locket?' Archie asked. 'I mean, she didn't visit you after she took you to the Fortesques, or ask how you were doing, or anything else, you said.'

'I don't know what she was,' Mary answered truthfully. She looked at the locket, clearly seeing how it had been worked back and forth until it snapped. She'd been given one heart-shaped half and Daniel the other. In hers was a picture of a young boy, her brother. In his, would be picture of her. The broken edge was still sharp. It seemed sharp enough to have easily cut Lorna Denbie.

Archie ran a finger across the jagged edge.

'Mary, how come she didn't have a cut on her palm?' he asked. 'She bled loads, but I didn't see even a bit of a cut. Then she talked about…' Archie hesitated. 'About the Ripper. She knew something about him… and why he ain't been around.'

'She knew something, all right. I thought she was afraid of something.'

'Maybe something went wrong, you know, during the exorcism… and that's what Mrs Denbie's afraid might happen to Lorna.'

Mary fell quiet. Danny Finch was still on her mind. Her dream had always been to find him and be reunited as a family again. But the worry was that he, like their parents, had died, and that was something she did not want to think about. She wondered if that was the reason he never tried to find her, and she rued the fact that she lacked the courage to try to discover the truth sooner. Now Lorna Denbie had a vision that he was in danger. From wherever he was, with whatever astral energy he possessed (a term she had read in a Penny Dreadful), Daniel Finch reached out across the void to touch Lorna Denbie's mind.

Mary shivered at the thought that mediums only spoke with the dead. But Danny wanted to be found, Lorna said. Surely that meant he was alive?

'He'd be eighteen now. I was always going to try and find Danny, and now I have to if he's in danger.' Mary chewed her lip and gazed longingly back in the direction of Berwick Street. 'I'd have paid her, Archie. I'm sure Lorna Denbie knew more than she was telling. But she seemed scared. Didn't she?'

They stood quietly on the pavement in Oxford Street, while the shoppers milled around them. Mary felt very small and insignificant, like a lost child, and the world seemed to be an awfully big place all of a sudden. Archie, perhaps sensing her feelings, hugged her, while people passed by and gave them no mind whatsoever.

'I've only two pictures of him, Archie. This one in my locket and the one my aunt gave me of the family. It ain't much, is it? I've got a day off next week. Will you come with me to see the Fortesques?'

'Need you ask?' Archie said.

'But first, this séance,' Mary said apprehensively, walking on. 'I've a bad feeling about that, Archie.' Her fingers tingled and she felt jittery. Although her mind tried to make sense of why she felt that way, it eluded her.

❦ *9* ❦

THE SÉANCE

THE WIND ROSE OVERNIGHT AS if in anticipation of the strangeness that Wednesday promised. It swirled and gusted and buffered the casements of the house in Holland Park. Windows rattled as the gale tried to force its way in, finding passage down chimneys and wailing an unearthly moan as it flew through the rooms. Half-opened doors slammed, fires flickered, and Mary tossed and turned in her bed, as her cat, Oscar, retreated to the security of the wardrobe and declined to leave.

Then from howling darkness came the forlorn cry of Daniel Finch, calling out to be found.

By morning, the gale had blown itself out, but it left a heavy, overcast sky that the sun could not pierce, and a perfectly still day without a hint of a breeze. Spring was temporarily abandoned and the dull, dismal morning rolled on inexorably towards noon.

At the stroke of the appointed hour, Mrs Denbie and her daughter arrived with their sullen-faced maid. They all wore high-necked black dresses, a colour most suited to the mood of the day. Mary watched in fascination as they went about their business, setting up the accoutrements they would need for the séance in practised silence. A crucifix and candelabra and various objects were placed on the dining table in the morning room. The curtains were drawn shut.

Only when Mrs Denbie finished patrolling the perimeter of the room, sprinkling Holy water and chanting some strange words, checking that the windows were secured and the door locked, was she satisfied that all was ready. She bade the participants sit. The lights were doused and a single candle lit and placed in the centre of the dining table. Flickering shadows washed the walls as the room descended into semi-darkness.

Mrs Denbie made it clear. They were sailing an ocean for which no map existed and she greatly feared for her daughter's well-being were Lorna ever to be lost on such a great expanse. Therefore, everyone must do whatever was asked of him or her, unreservedly, unquestioningly.

At the head of the table sat Lorna Denbie. She wore white cotton gloves. She sat on a comfortable recliner while the others occupied straight-backed dining room chairs. On her left sat her mother, followed by Mrs Grady, Mr Venables, Archie (who arrived uninvited, much to Mary's relief), and finally Mary, sitting next to

Lorna to complete the circle. Away from them, in a corner, sat the Denbies' maid.

Cook refused to take part, taking Ella and Fortune with her. Both girls rushed home from school, but now they were there, Fortune became reticent. This was voodoo, the little West Indian girl whispered to Mary, like the wicked thing that followed her father from his home in Haiti, and it was that thing, a Jumbie, that struck him dead.

Mrs Denbie bound her daughter to the chair with a silken cord.

'It is a precaution,' she explained, 'so she cannot harm herself, or us, should she become possessed.'

Then they held hands.

'The circle is not to be broken,' Mrs Denbie cautioned, 'on no account, no matter what happens, no matter what you see. The universal energy must be allowed to flow freely between us. Only a spirit or Lorna can ask us to disengage. To do otherwise risks my daughter's sanity, if not her life.'

Lorna's grasp of Mary's hand was light, yet firm. She gave an easy smile to the gathering. Closing her eyes and taking a deep breath, she exhaled and seemed to relax into herself.

'I shall summon the grey woman,' Lorna said, 'and return her from where she came. Only when she names herself can her power be broken.'

First they recited the Lord's Prayer, and then Lorna Denbie's thin, penetrating voice spoke Psalm 27:

'The Lord is the stronghold of my life…'

Mary shivered with the oddness of the occasion. The only sounds she could hear were her breathing, the quickening pulse of her heart in her ears, and Lorna Denbie softly reciting some chant. She repeated it incessantly, her voice becoming neither louder nor quieter, a constant humming drone.

Soon, Mary became aware of the occasional murmurings from beyond the window, faraway and distant sounds of the real world. This room had changed into someplace strange. The apprehension she'd felt standing with Archie on Oxford Street came to her once again and she raised her eyes.

In the weak, flickering light, Mary noticed all those around the table had lowered their gazes. She was aware that the Denbies' maid was watching from a darkened corner, the candle's dancing light catching a shine in her eyes. Mary lowered her vision.

Beside her, Lorna still mumbled her strange chant. Then her incantations grew louder. Mary did not understand the words. She thought they might be Latin, but she could not be sure. But they sounded insistent, like a voice calling out into the night to be heard. Mary shivered in trepidation of who might answer its call.

A sweet smell filled her nose, and she felt Lorna tense.

'Something is present,' Mrs Denbie whispered.

Lorna gasped loudly; there was a sharp intake of breath. Mary flicked her eyes up in astonishment and felt the girl's grip tighten. The sinews in Lorna's face and neck bulged as she strained against the silken cord. Then a groan, like a deep primaeval agony, issued from her mouth. Immediately, the hairs on Mary's arms prickled. Fearful for the girl, she grasped her hand tighter.

An instant later, a small voice started singing. A child's voice, distant and lonely, like a soul lost in a wilderness, rose above their heads in a piping chant.

'The Grand Old Duke of York, he had ten thousand men...'

Mary's eyes flicked right and left, searching for the voice that seemed to be both near and far. Mixed in with the voice came laughter. She tried to follow the sounds, but they were everywhere at once.

'Who are you?' Lorna shouted. Her face contorted and she winced as if something stabbed her. She gulped air like a drowning man raised to the surface. 'Show yourself.'

'... he marched them up to the top of the hill...'

'Speak!' Lorna demanded.

'Wouldn't you like to know?' A voice, guttural and evil spoke from out of the darkness. 'Wouldn't you like to know?' it repeated, becoming a laugh.

'Who are you? Name yourself!' Lorna commanded.

'... when they were up, they were up...'

'Why should I, when you know who I am.'

'Tell us,' Lorna said.

A burst of hideous laughter filled the room. Mary started—something brushed against her and she flinched and gasped. Her eyes flicked around as a cold sweat wetted her skin.

A noxious smell permeated the air and burned her nose. At the same moment, she felt Lorna struggling. She tightened her grip, fearful of letting go. The girl's face contorted in agony and she groaned as the voice cried out.

'Name me, if you dare!'

'... *and when they were down, they were down...*'

'Name yourself!' Lorna shouted.

'... *and when they were only half-way up...*'

'I need no name.'

'... *they were neither up nor...*'

There was a dreadful cry from Lorna. Immediately, the singing stopped and fearful whispers erupted, first to Mary's right, then left, and then all around.

'I am the Grey Lady,' screamed a voice, and immediately the whispers fled.

'Name yourself!' Lorna demanded. 'Or leave in the name of our Lord. You have no business here.' But her voice was no more than a frightened plea.

Mary forced her gaze up. Some unspeakable agony gripped Lorna. The girl shook and trembled. She pulled and struggled to free herself from the cord that held her tight against the chair, while around her, the voice boomed.

'You have summoned me from my sleep. My curse is upon you.' Hollow and deep, it spat oaths and invectives and cursed Mrs Grady by name. 'I will burn your house to the ground. I will bring down my mistress's vengeance on you, none will be spared my wrath. My breath is death—'

'Stop this! Stop this!' Mrs Denbie screamed. 'Lorna, desist. Wake. Wake, now!'

Lorna arched backwards, her sinews rippled and tightened against the cord, her eyes rolled. She trembled violently, then suddenly went limp and flopped down like a rag doll as if exhausted.

Fearful of letting go, Mary clutched Lorna's hand. The tortured face of Professor Cavendish filled her mind. She could feel Archie's hand, clammy with sweat, and Lorna's grip, still light but firm. The moment hung heavily in the air that was scented with the sweet smell of violets. It became deathly quiet, and it seemed that even outside, everything was silent. It was as if time stood still, unmoving, resolutely refusing to advance a single second. Then Lorna's lips moved.

'Tis the last rose of summer,
Left blooming alone;
All her lovely companions
Are faded and gone...

She was singing softly, but her voice was deep, like that of a man. Her head lolled to one side. An odd grin broke apart her thin ruby lips. She was watching Mrs Grady, a mischievous look through half-closed eyes. The old lady flinched so violently that the table shook. Then to Mary's surprise, Mrs Grady's started to mimed the words.

> *'No flower of her kindred,*
> *No rose-bud is nigh,*
> *To reflect back her blushes…*
> *In my Janie's eye.'*

Lorna chuckled over the last line.

'Patrick?' Mrs Grady whispered. Her eyes fell on to Lorna.

'Do not break the circle,' Mrs Denbie cautioned, sensing Mrs Grady was about to rise.

'Who are you?' Lorna Denbie asked in her squeaky voice.

Mary squinted as a mist, like a river fog, invaded the room. It grew around her, and she blinked to penetrate it. Something was forming in the mist, coalescing, taking shape before her eyes.

As she watched, she stiffened. Daniel Finch was walking through the curtains. He was smiling and his hand was extended, reaching out to her like he did in her dream.

To her horror, he began to change. His face, wracked with pain, morphed and shimmered. From the front of his shirt, blood spouted, red flowers blooming and spreading across the white linen.

He scowled at her. 'Why didn't you look for me?' he demanded.

Her pounding heart drowned his voice. Her stomach tightened and she gasped for breath as he slowly started to fade, going pale and transparent in much the same way Tom Norris had done all those months ago, and disappeared as the river fog evaporated.

'Now, what sort of trouble have you got yourself into, my beautiful Rose?' Lorna Denbie said in the same smiling voice that sung the song. 'Messing with things you shouldn't be messing with, Rosie, just like you, isn't it? Now, remember what I told you in Murray Finnegan's Inn that night in Galway? Aye, Rosie, you'll not be rid of me that easily. And that thing, threatening you.'

Mrs Grady was stunned into silence. Her mouth hung loosely open and jabbered incoherently.

'And look at you, Tobias Venables. Now, man, that's a fine, handsome suit if ever I saw one.' The voice laughed pleasantly. As if in a silent dream, Mary saw Mr Venables's eyes drag across the faces towards the reclining figure of Lorna, who beamed broadly and wickedly at him.

'Mum!' Archie whispered.

Mary's eyes shot around. Archie's face was drenched

in sweat. He was watching with a vacant stare some invisible figure in front of him. He attempted to rise, but fell back into his seat. Mr Venables blinked several times as if he, too, was seeing someone standing behind Lorna.

A trickle of blood ran from Mrs Grady's nose and Mary saw her slip down. To her surprise, Mrs Denbie was no longer holding her daughter's hand. Nor was she holding Lorna's. Quietly and deftly Lorna released her grip without Mary noticing. The girl, instead, clasped her arms around her mother's shoulders. She shook as a fit of trembling gripped her.

All around them came the whispers once more.

A cold breeze swirled. The Denbies' maid was pulling wide the blinds and opening the windows. Light flooded the room. The whispers, as if banished by the light, grew feeble, leaving, vanishing, while from outside came the sharp chirping of birds, the neighing of horses and the clip-clop of their hooves on the cobbles.

It was over.

10

LORNA DENBIE'S VISION

With the help of the Denbies' maid, Mary manhandled the semi-conscious Lorna to a sofa in the morning room. The girl muttered incessantly.

Mrs Denbie explained, 'She is still communing with the spirit. She will not rouse until they let her go. It is best I tend her alone.'

'Is it the Grey Lady?' Mary asked.

Mrs Denbie did not answer, but her face betrayed her fears. She knelt beside her daughter, and as Mary turned away, she overheard the woman's soft cry.

'Lorna, why, oh, why did I allow you to come here?'

The odd event left Mary confused and afraid. Her brother, as plain as the nose on her face, had been standing in front of her. She tried to make sense of it, but time seemed to be moving strangely and she was unsettled.

She turned to Archie. The boy's face was pale. She wondered what had frightened him so.

Cook cradled Mrs Grady and dabbed the blood from her nose. Though the greyness left her cheeks and the old lady could sit up, she seemed far away and distracted, and ignored Cook's many questions.

When the Denbies' maid collected all the items used in the séance, Mary helped her take them to the front door. She was pleased to be doing something useful, happy to be out of the room and away from the others, to be someplace where she could think.

Having finished her task, everything placed neatly by the front door, Mary sat on the stairs. Oscar, as if sensing her troubled mind, wandered up to sit beside her.

'I don't understand any of this, Oz,' she said. The cat gave a low hiss, jumped down and started to snuffle, crawling inside Mrs Denbie's bag. 'Hey! Get your nose out of there. There ain't no food there.' As she dragged him out, he seemed disturbed and sneezed. 'I saw Danny.' She blinked back her tears. 'But he was all bloody. And he asked me why I didn't try to find him. But I was going to. I really was. I didn't mean to let him down—'

Suddenly, Oscar hissed again as if angry at her. His fur prickled, his back arched. He turned. His eyes were dark and wild, and he slashed at Mary. Then the cat was away, rushing up the stairs and along the corridor in an untamed panic.

Mary winced and wrapped a handkerchief around her arm where the cat clawed her.

'Daft animal,' she whispered. She became aware of the sounds from the morning room. Mrs Denbie and her daughter were speaking. Mary slipped back inside to listen.

Lorna looked drained. Hesitantly, as if trying to make sense of her words, she related a vision given to her by the spirits just before she was released. She spoke fearfully.

'I saw death, in all its horrid forms, stoop to kiss the face of the water.' Lorna's childlike voice settled uneasily on her listeners. Her words were from someone beyond her years, as if it were he, the spirit she raised, who was speaking through her. But now she was no longer possessed. 'I felt such overwhelming hopelessness; such despair, the gravity of which, should it have grasped my heart, would have stopped it beating as it did theirs. How they fought. How they bargained with their god to be spared. Their eyes betrayed their fears. But none were spared. The water that claimed them listened not to a single plea, but sowed the ocean floor with their bones.'

A shudder shook Lorna and caused Mrs Denbie to hold her daughter. She rocked her gently until the trembling passed. Lorna drew her face deeper into her hood until only her eyes could be seen, and continued in her soft voice. She was looking directly at Mrs Grady.

'But fire burned within the souls of those that

drowned that day and they cried out for vengeance. They cursed him that lured them there with false promises of wealth. They carried him away with them, just as he carried them away in a ship that bore your name.

'Who were they? What a terrible fate they suffered, that in each and every eye should reside the image of he who sang that song. Mark my words: perdition will not be denied his soul until recompense is made.' Her voice cracked.

A wave of anger reddened Cook's face. She whispered, 'Patrick Grady? It is he you speak of? This is a sin. Not another word of that foul blasphemy.' She scowled at the Denbies. 'I want you out of this house, do you hear? This minute!'

'It is still my house, Eileen,' Mrs Grady said softly and laid a trembling hand on Cook. 'Go on, child. If there is more, pray tell. I shall listen.'

Lorna eased back against her mother and fell quiet. Mrs Denbie whispered into her ear and nodded for her to speak.

'But it was also love I felt,' Lorna continued timidly. 'His love reached out and bridged the gap.' Her face looked puzzled and she closed her eyes tightly and whispered, 'Two survived and live.' She shook her head, not understanding the words, and looked at Mrs Grady quizzically. 'You and another.'

'I?' Mrs Grady said. 'You speak of the death of my husband, child. Of that I am certain. How could I survive something that I was not a part of? I have survived no shipwreck. Who is this other?'

'But I do not know,' Lorna said. She closed her eyes and again fell deeply into thought. 'Forgive me. I do not *see* things as such, but *feel* them. I *felt* two. You, Mrs Grady, were one. Your aura is strong. But the other was faint and I did not know her. Yet she is as much a part of the story as are you.'

'She?' Mrs Grady asked. 'Of whom do you speak, child, tell me?'

'Why, I do not know, only that there was death in her face. She has been wronged and seeks justice.'

'The Grey Lady?' Mary asked.

Lorna looked up in surprise. She gripped her mother tightly and said, 'No, it is not she. But this other has lost something precious, and in doing so has lost herself. I heard a voice cry, "Siobhan—he who had gone before, who was lost, but still is", and the voice was hushed—'

Cook turned to Mr Venables, and at the same moment, Mrs Grady flinched.

'What game is this?' Mr Venables demanded. 'Speak plainly and not in riddles.'

He leant forward so quickly that Lorna shrank back in fear and bowed her head to hide her face. Her mother glared angrily at the Butler.

'The voice said *she* came before you, yet she was also after you, and now she is with you,' Lorna said quietly.

Mrs Grady reached out to place a hand on the Butler.

Her eyes held a wild stare, but seemingly saw nothing. It was not unlike the way she'd looked on the journey to Charing Cross Hospital.

Lorna stuttered an apology and whispered, 'I cannot explain, nor can I tell you more. Forgive me, Mrs Grady. I do not know the meaning of my visions. I can only report them. I am sorry. The task I came to do I, could not accomplish. I could not get the Grey Lady to name herself. I could not send her away. Perhaps you were right, after all, Mama, and I am not yet strong enough.'

'I must take my daughter home,' Mrs Denbie said abruptly, and she called her maid over.

Rose Grady stirred as if waking from a dream. She looked lost, but when she found herself, she nodded.

Mary helped the Denbies find a cab. Lorna leant heavily against her mother as the maid fussed over the exhausted girl. When Mary returned to the house, a heated argument was taking place in the morning room.

'He swore to me, Eileen, on our wedding night in Murray Finnegan's Inn,' Mrs Grady was saying, 'that neither heaven nor hell would ever part us. He would find me, even if he searched the world a dozen times over. I have told no one that. No one! In thirty years, not a soul. Tell me, how could anyone have known that?'

Cook scowled and shook her head. 'I do not know. But it is not God's purpose to tease you like this. There has to be another explanation.'

'I saw Patrick,' Mrs Grady said determinedly and

Cook crossed herself. 'I saw him in that young girl's face, and then I saw him, just as you sit here, I saw him in all his fineries. And he sang that damn song and changed the last line, like he always did to make fun with me. How many people know that, Eileen? No one but Patrick and me.' There were tears in Mrs Grady's eyes.

Cook sat uncomfortably. Her angry voice boomed out to the Butler: 'And I suppose you saw something as well.'

Mr Venables dropped his gaze and took a deep breath as if to compose himself, then said, 'Patrick! As I live and breathe, it was he I saw.'

Cook clucked in disbelief. There was a look on her face as if she wanted to grab them and shake them for believing in ghosts like frightened children.

Instead, she demanded, 'And what did I hear about Siobhan?' Mrs Grady's face was closed. 'Rosie, I wish you'd stop messing with things that you know nothing about. Ungodly things as well. Now, what did she say about Siobhan?'

No one answered.

'And the wreck?' Cook asked.

Still, no one answered, and Cook huffed angrily.

Mary was confused. Like all the others, she had seen something. She went to stand beside Archie. He, too, was troubled and silent. She took his hand and the boy stirred. His eyes blinked several times as he held back some tears, and before Mary could speak, he answered her unspoken question.

'Mum,' he said simply. 'I saw Mum,' and fell quiet.

'Danny,' Mary said in answer to his silence. 'But he was hurt. He was bleeding and he was angry at me. Archie, is he dead? Is that why I saw him? Just yesterday, that girl said he was in danger. But she only speaks to the dead. I don't understand what it means. Does it mean Danny's dead? Was that why he was angry at me?'

She struggled to hold back her tears. But all Archie could do was shake his head.

11

MARY'S FINDINGS

THERE WAS a strange atmosphere in the house for the rest of the day. It was as if no one dared speak. But when they did, they shouted.

Cook's voice filled the kitchen with fury.

'She's dead,' she yelled. 'Siobhan Fitzwilliam is forty years dead. The famine claimed her and her child. Why did that girl speak of her?'

'I do not know,' Mr Venables shouted back. 'But tell me, how did that girl know all of those things? Few, other than Rosie, know them.'

When they saw Mary standing in the pantry, they fell quiet. But a fit of fierce anger smouldered in Cook's eyes that could not be hidden. She turned and glared at Fortune standing by the door.

'Fortune Dubois, you speak of Jumbies and those

heathen ghost things once more to Mrs Grady and I swear…' she ground her teeth and left the threat hanging as Fortune ran from the kitchen.

That evening, Mary sat quietly on her bed. She had seen her brother as clear as day, but was it Danny's ghost? Mediums and clairvoyants only spoke to the dead. That much she knew.

She was impatient for her day off. The wait, though, would be frustrating. If she did nothing, if she brooded on her concerns, she felt she would go mad. Her blood was up.

Mary considered how it all begun with the expedition Mrs Grady sponsored, that happened before she joined the household. Somehow, the Denbies, the Grey Lady, the deaths of all those people, and the strange visions everyone saw earlier were connected. She had to find out more.

She stormed out of her bedroom. It was Mr Venables's habit to keep old newspapers, which were used to light the fires. He had stored a good year's worth of them, and she removed the last four months' to her bedroom. With Fortune's help, she carefully combed through the articles, cutting out any relating to the Cavendish expedition and the Grey Lady.

The next day, when Archie came to see her, the articles were all in neat rows on the bed. Archie apologised for his behaviour the day before, for his silence and leaving so quickly without any explanation. It was less his behaviour that troubled him, Mary knew, but the vision of his mother. After all, her own vision had been equally troubling.

'So, what's all this, then?' he asked, clearly not wishing to speak about his concerns.

'My research.' Mary waved a hand across the newspaper cuttings. 'It's what Mr Holmes says: "You can't theorise until you have data, otherwise you'll twist facts to suit the theory, instead of theory to suit the facts".'

'Mr Holmes again!' Archie chuckled.

'Laugh all you want. If it's good enough for Mr Holmes, it's good enough for me,' Mary said. 'Now, listen!'

Archie saluted.

'This is the picture Mrs Grady showed me. *The day they awoke death,* she said. It was taken when they opened the tomb.' She gave Archie the photograph of the expedition members. 'Well, four of them died in England, and the fifth one vanished soon after the tomb was opened. Mr Venables said a crocodile got him when he went bathing in the river, but his body was never found. He was the first one to die.'

Her eyes were bright and lively. Archie leant back and said, 'Go on, *Missus Holmes.'*

'Well, it's all pretty strange stuff,' Mary pointed to one of the articles on her bed. 'Take Mr Sinclair, for instance. He was the surveyor on the expedition, you know, taking measurements and such so they could locate the tombs. He died soon after they arrived back in England. He fell from a train. Witnesses said he was agitated, almost hysterical. Apparently, he started running up the railway tracks as if he was being chased, and before anyone could get to him, a train going the other way hit him. But he was a railwayman. That was his business. It's where he made his fortune.'

'Wasn't he an Egyptologist?' Archie asked.

'That's the thing,' Mary said thoughtfully, her brows creasing. 'Apart from Professor Cavendish, they all did different things. It's only this archaeology lark they all had in common.'

'All right for some,' Archie sniffed.

'Then there was Mr Chambers.'

'The one who thought he could fly?' Archie picked up Chambers's obituary and quickly scanned it before Mary spoke again.

'That's the point—he could. He was a student of some German bloke, Otto Lilienthal who they called the flying man. He had a machine called a glider, and with it, he flew. Once, apparently, Mr Chambers had himself strapped to a massive kite and it took him hundreds of feet up. Anyway, Mr Chambers was following in Otto's footstep, as it were, and—'

'Jumped from a church tower, it says here.'

Mary smiled a yes.

'He was going on and on about being able to soar like the birds when he jumped, like he'd gone mad. Then there's Mr Barnet. He was ex-Royal Navy and an excellent swimmer, but he drowned in a lake you could wade in. Now his expertise was in something called a rebreathing apparatus.'

Archie looked over, and Mary shrugged and found an article that had a diagram of this invention.

'It's a sack-like thing, with holes for your eyes covered in glass. You place it over your head, and it's attached by a tube to another thing that has air in it,' Mary said vaguely, pointing at the illustration. 'With it, you can stay underwater longer than you can do normally by just holding your breath. He was an expert and the Navy was interested.'

'It's all good and that, Mary, and all pretty odd, I'll give you, but—'

'Listen,' Mary interrupted and Archie smiled broadly, seeing her enthusiasm. 'Lastly, there was Professor Cavendish. He thought Mrs Grady was the Egyptian priestess, Nefrusheri, and then he died. He *was* an archaeologist and Ancient Egypt *was* his passion. Now, there are two things.'

Mary's face became serious.

'The first is that the Grey Lady was present somewhere at all their deaths. She was seen on the train with Mr Sinclair, in the church with Mr Chambers, across the lake from Mr Barnet and at Professor Cavendish's bedside. Even I saw her there. Lots of people told the papers what they'd seen, but the reporters couldn't find hide nor hair of her. Secondly, the manner of their deaths had some connection to whatever it was that interested them… more than the archaeology, I mean.'

Archie's brow furrowed a question.

'Sinclair and trains. Chambers and flying. Barnet and water. And Cavendish and Nefrusheri,' Mary said.

'So, what's any of that got to do with brass tacks?'

'It's curious, don't you think? Each death connected with something they liked or did. Coincidence, or what?'

'What about all that other stuff the medium spoke about?' Archie asked. 'Sinking and drownings, and false promises, and … what was her name? Siobhan?'

A wide smile broke Mary's face.

'Patrick Grady was married to Siobhan Fitzwilliam before he met Rose Grady,' she announced. Archie looked over as if to ask how she knew that. 'I have a spy. No one ever notices Fortune, so she can just stand and listen—she hears all sorts. Apparently, Siobhan and Patrick had a child. When Patrick was in jail for a robbery, Siobhan and her child died. This was during the famine in Ireland. Cook knew Siobhan and Mr Venables met her a couple of times. Years after she died, Patrick married Mrs Grady.'

'And the other stuff?'

'That!' Mary said heavily. 'Fortune heard how Patrick Grady made his money. The telling ain't pretty. He was a smuggler, amongst other things. His real money came from running guns and other contraband to America before the civil war over there—'

'A gun runner?' Archie said sharply. 'I wonder what else he smuggled?'

'That don't bear thinking about,' Mary said. There were things, far worse than guns that Patrick Grady may have been involved in, that she did not want to consider. 'The story is that a Royal Navy frigate chased his ship, the Jane Rose.' She nodded. 'Yes, the one Lorna Denbie mentioned, and it ran aground during a storm. Everyone drowned—Patrick, his partner, the crew—everyone. Horrible, ain't it?' Mary shivered when she imagined their fate. 'That's what Lorna Denbie saw.'

'And Mrs Grady married *him?*' Archie shook his head in disbelief.

'I don't think she knew then what she knows now,' Mary said softly. 'Believe me, she doesn't approve one bit. And she uses her money to help others as much as she can. It's not like she's keeping it all to herself, is it? All those charities she supports.'

'And her husband's soul is trapped, never to go one way or the other,' Archie sniffed. 'Serves him right! I tell you, Mary, when I go, I'd like to know which direction my soul's heading—up or down—and I'd make damn sure it goes the right way.'

'Poor Mrs Grady,' Mary said. 'She's locked herself away, she's so worried. She's been carrying this around for months—the death of all those people and now that séance. It must be driving her mad. She looks all done in. She was muttering to herself all yesterday. She even said how nice it'd be to die. I'm sure that's what I heard. She's changed from when I first came to work here.'

Archie fell quiet and looked concerned.

'What's wrong?' she asked.

'I know I said I don't believe in ghosts and stuff like that, Mary,' he said. 'But I saw her as I sees you now. I saw Mum.'

Almost immediately, he dropped his head, and his face flushed red in embarrassment. The séance stirred up so many ghosts. They were all knocking and wanting to be heard and remembered.

Once again, Archie shook his head, 'I mean...' he said, and was quiet. 'Come on,' he said brusquely and a shadow seemed to pass from his face. 'Now you've got all this information, what's your theory, *Missus Holmes?*'

Before she could speak, a rap on the door silenced her. An anxious Fortune leaned in.

'Miss Mary,' she said hesitantly. 'Mr Venables gave me this letter to give to Mistress,' and she held out an unsealed envelope.

'Well, give it to her,' Mary said.

Fortune hopped from one leg to the other, her face screwed up in anguish.

'It's just that I think Mistress is mad at me for speaking about Jumbies and I... I...'

Mary sighed. 'Give it here,' she said.

Mrs Grady was in bed. The curtains were drawn, and although an oil lamp had been lit, the wick was turned low and the room was in shadow. Even so, Mary noticed how sickly pale Mrs Grady looked. Her eyes were red and swollen. On her insistence, Mary read the letter aloud.

Mrs Frances Denbie

22 Berwick Street

Soho

By hand.

Dear Mrs Grady,

I trust you are in good health. I write with regards to recent events.

I am aware that there was no satisfactory conclusion to our business, and indeed, that it may have raised more questions than it answered. I regret that I cannot put your mind to rest. The visions that Lorna 'sees' are never as clear as one would want them to be. While they may be confusing, I can, nevertheless, assure you of their truthfulness.

I had hoped that her visions would be comforting, but, forgive me, we came to provide a different service and were unable to fulfil that responsibility.

Lorna has informed me that while you are still in danger, the Grey Lady seeks another first. Who that is, she does not know. I apologise. It must be of no comfort to read this. However, she may still be obstructed. To that end, please accept the small gift within. It is a crucifix that belonged to Pope Innocent X and I believe it will protect you until such time as the spirit can be returned whence it came.

I would also like to thank you for the generosity of your payment for our services. However, you have compensated us in excess of our agreement, and we have reimbursed the difference.

Yours sincerely,

FRANCES DENBIE

The hand-delivered envelope contained a folded five-pound note and a small, plain-but-elegant, golden cross, no more than an inch tall, on a chain. Mary gave them to Mrs Grady. The old lady slipped the crucifix around her neck and went to her writing desk to fashion a reply. Mary assured her Archie would deliver it on his way home.

JANE GRADY
The Rose Garden
Holland Park

.

DEAR MRS DENBIE,

PLEASE CONVEY TO YOUR DAUGHTER MY GRATITUDE FOR her endeavour. It was greatly appreciated. My thanks for your kind gift. It is of comfort and I wear it now.

I HAVE RETURNED YOU THE EXCESS PAYMENT, PLEASE accept the amount as given for your services.

YOURS SINCERELY,

JANE R GRADY

12

THE SARCOPHAGUS OF
NEFRUSHERI

THAT NIGHT WAS a restless one where the spirits of her mother and father were almost tangible in uneasy dreams. The Grey Lady was there also. Her strange pale face, featureless but for her hollow skull-like eyes, awoke Mary in a cold sweat well before dawn.

When she came downstairs, Mary was surprised. The household was up early and Mrs Grady was already breakfasting. Though her face was bright, her eyes betrayed the strain of the last few days, the months since the first séance, and the deaths of the members of the expedition. She was wearing the cross and, Mary assumed, she felt protected by whatever power it possessed. It was that, perhaps, which appeared to comfort her.

Now that the mistress was up and about, and seemingly her old self again, a sea change overtook the household. Thoughts of the last few days were banished and everyone was busy, not least of all, Cook, who bustle and fussed, happy once more.

'I shall be going to the British Museum,' Mrs Grady announced brightly. 'They will be opening the sarcophagus of the high priestess, Nefrusheri, and I intend to be there.'

'I suppose the press being there has nothing to do with it,' Cook said mischievously.

'Shame on you, Eileen! You have a wicked mind. They will be there to record the occasion only.' She winked with a smile on her lips. 'But I can see it doing some good for the women's movement. Now, Mary, how would you like to come along with me? We will need a man to accompany us as well. That will be your friend, Archie. We shall pick him up along the way.'

Mary was jittery with anticipation. She was rather looking forward to seeing what a mummy really looked like when the lid was taken off the sarcophagus. Would it be all wrapped in linen? Would things crawl out from between the bandages? She giggled. Would it rise up and walk as one did in a story she once read? She had an image of the museum people running and hiding in fright as Nefrusheri walked amongst them.

Lady Mary Finch steeled herself. She aimed the revolver at the mummy's heart and squeezed the trigger. To her horror, the creature walked on, oblivious to the barking of the gun and the terrible wounds it caused.

Fire, the Lady realised, was her only weapon against this beast from the grave…

A tug on her dress startled Mary from her daydream.

'Miss Mary,' Fortune whispered, her furtive eyes flicking left and right as she looked around, seemingly concerned that no one should be nearby. 'Take this, it'll keep you and Mistress safe,' and she surreptitiously passed over a small, crude handmade doll wrapped in coarse hessian. A bright red upside-down heart-shaped cloth was sewn to the front. 'It'll scare the Jumbies if they try anything.'

She continued to glance around apprehensively as she pressed the doll into Mary's hand.

'Fortune—'

'No, Miss Mary, it will. Me know these things,' the girl said desperately. 'I've said good prayers over it all night. It'll keep you and Mrs Grady safe. See, it's got some of your hair and some of Mistress's as well, so it knows who to protect.'

On each side of the head were glued two small locks of hair—the unmistakable red of Mrs Grady and the mousey brown that was Mary's.

'Where'd you get these?' Mary asked in amazement.

'Last night,' Fortune gazed up with wide, innocent eyes.

'Last night? What are you saying? You clipped a bit of our hair? When we were asleep?' The young girl's face was unsmilingly serious, her eyes deep set and solemn. 'You sneaked into our rooms—?'

'It'll protect you from Jumbies, Miss Mary.' Fortune said it as if it were common knowledge. 'Please, believe me, I had to do it. It's not just Mistress the Jumbie wants, it's you as well. That's what that lady meant about it wanting to kill another.'

Mary was about to ask how she knew that, then she understood—Fortune must have read Mrs Denbie's letter.

'I know it will protect you both,' Fortune continued. 'It has so much goodness in it because I prayed so much, nothing will get past it.' Her eyes flicked around. Cook was walking towards them. 'Please, Miss Mary, hide it before Cook sees,' she said anxiously. 'Please, Miss Mary, please. She don't believe and it won't work unless you believe, and I know you do.'

Flustered, Mary quickly slipped the doll into her pocket. She could imagine Cook's indignation if she saw it, and the blue fit she would have if she knew that Fortune entered Mrs Grady's bedroom to snip a lock of hair.

'Fortune Dubois,' Cook grumped, 'how many times have I got to tell you: light the kitchen stove first thing in the morning, and put the kettle on for tea.'

'Sorry, Cook,' Fortune said, rushing off.

'It's too late for that, young lady,' Cook called after her. 'Now, get your exercise book. Ella's waiting for you.

And what did she want, Mary? Wanting to skive school again, I suppose.'

Mary smiled a lie. 'Oh! Just gabbing.'

'That girl's been acting strange ever since those two hussies left,' Cook said angrily. But Mary knew she was more upset with the two hussies—the Denbies—than Fortune.

Cook turned away and did not see the young girl hiding behind a chair. Fortune fixed Mary with a deep, dark gaze. She mumbled some inaudible words as she held a small crucifix tightly in her fingers. A shiver ran up Mary's spine. She felt for the doll. Her fingers closed round it, feeling the coarseness of the hessian and the silk of the hair. Then, seeing Mrs Grady approaching, she pushed the doll firmly down inside her pocket. When she glanced around, the maid was running down the corridor to the back of the house.

Mary and Mrs Grady left soon after. For the entire journey, Mary's mind swirled around the odd conversation with Fortune. It left her apprehensive. It was only after they had taken tea with the Dibbles and started out towards Bloomsbury with Archie that her thoughts cleared sufficiently for her to look forward to the occasion.

They alighted from the carriage at the grand steps leading up to the British Museum. Mary walked with barely concealed delight to the basement where the artefacts of the expedition lay. She travelled through rooms and rooms of dark gloominess that, not surprisingly, reeked of knowledge and age. She marvelled at the shelves, cases and racks that populated the spaces—dust-covered statues, still-crated treasures of long-forgotten civilizations, all waiting in saintly silence, as they had done for centuries past, for the precious wisdom of the ages to be prised from their unspeaking mouths. In these rabbit warrens, Ancient Greece mixed with Babylon, watched over by the dynasties of China, spied on by the treasures from Darien and places that were barely remembered in living memory.

She felt her heart catch in her throat. Five thousand years' worth of histories resided quietly, peacefully, disorderly below the streets of Bloomsbury, awaiting the pronouncements by ermine-robed professors as to the meaning of the runes and cartouches that puzzled and perplexed generations past. The blood that built king-doms, ruled Empires long since fallen and commanded the destinies of millions, now strived to tell once more of how great they were, to anyone who may care to listen.

Yet history lives, so the press would have everyone believe, citing the notoriety surrounding Mrs Grady's Egyptian collection. The papers had not been slow in making connections between the recent deaths of the expedition members and the curse of Nefrusheri, sparing no column inches in expounding their theories. The wronged priestess had reached across the vast span of time and across countless dunes of the Sahara to wreak vengeance on those who defiled her and her mistress. She shall have her due, and none shall be spared her wrath, the papers mocked.

The sarcophagus of Nefrusheri lay on several strong tables around which had been cleared a wide space. A block and tackle, suspended from the ceiling, was attached to the lid. Mr Julian Barclay, the Museum's curator, a learned look inhabiting his face, posed self-importantly with Mrs Grady. They were to have their photograph taken beside the coffin. The experts who were to examine the remains were arranged around the stone casket, seemingly according to rank. Mrs Grady, the eminent sponsor, stood prominent amongst them at the front. The press stood back at a respectful distance, cameras on tripods, awaiting the moment Nefrusheri would be revealed, their faces burning bright with morbid anticipation.

'Gentlemen,' Mr Barclay's tenor voice blustered with pride, 'she has lain in darkness undisturbed for three and a half thousand years. Great Rome rose and fell, Europe descended into a Dark Age, Kublai Khan conquered and ruled China, and countless wars have ravaged the world, and in all that time, not a single eye has beheld her. Had not the late Professor Cavendish found her, she may well have rested for yet another three and a half thousand years—lost and forgotten, perhaps never to be found. We are privileged to be the first eyes to see her in over three millennia. Bear witness to the great Nefrusheri!'

He raised his arm.

'Take the strain, gentlemen,' someone shouted.

Mary, standing to one side with Archie, felt an electric tingle run along her skin as she saw the ropes tighten and begin to lift the lid. The beam holding the pulley groaned with the strain and dust motes flew down, flecking the air. A hush descended.

With a hiss and a sigh, the seal broke. A noxious smell mixed with the sweetness of violets wafted into the air. The representatives of the press murmured softly. The deep hum of wonder rose and fell away into quiet.

Slowly, the lid rose. Higher and higher it went to reveal a container richly decorated, painted with gesso, resin and chalk powder, intricate designs with madder, indigo and ochre. Osiris, the god of the underworld, guarded it with painted eyes.

With slow care, the lid was swung away and light fell on Nefrusheri in her cartonnage, bedecked in her funeral mask and armour of worked gold. She lay resplendent in her glory, her long night ended.

'Behold Nefrusheri, high priestess to Queen Hatshepsut,' Mr Barclay announced.

The cameras clicked. With a whoosh, magnesium powder flashed the brilliance of the sun and smoke clouded the ceiling. A cheer went up. Hands clapped. Voices, raised in compliments, echoed around the basement.

But even as the pressmen cheered, a dark mist clouded their faces.

There was a moment of silence, then Mrs Grady screamed a hideous wail that could turn the blood to ice. She flinched backwards in terror. Almost at once, there came the howl of a wild animal from behind the gathered newsmen. The long baying echoed off the walls, growing louder, and panic broke out.

Screaming and shouting, the reporters clutched their faces and gazed wild-eyed all round them. Cameras and tripods were dashed to the floor. Some tried to run, but collapsed in shivering heaps, curling up with hands over their heads. The same horror overtook those holding the pulley ropes. They released their burden and the coffin lid crashed to the ground beside the long-dead priestess.

Mary gasped in disbelief. Blinking to clear her vision she beheld the ragged mummy rising slowly from the coffin. Its vacant gaze fixed a deadly stare on her mistress. But Mrs Grady's eyes were elsewhere. She was looking beyond the crowd of panicking pressmen towards a figure deep inside the shadows who was pointing at her.

There behind the crowd, shimmering, glimmering, stood the Grey Lady. Her veil was raised, her face, skull-like white with two dark hollow sockets for eyes, and death in all its horror surrounded her.

'Defiler! Defiler!' the Grey Lady cried. 'My vengeance will fall on thee.'

13

THE BREATH OF DEATH

AT THE SIGHT of the Grey Lady, a sickness welled in Mary's stomach. She started out towards her mistress; her feet, however, refused to move and she was shivering with fear. The mummy was walking amongst the newsmen. All around her, the shadows thicken.

'Archie,' Mary screamed, 'help Mrs Grady.' But the boy was standing stock-still, wide eyes fixed on the coffin. Like her, he too was frozen to the spot.

Fortune's voice flooded her swirling mind: '*I know it will protect you both.*' Mary's cold fingers tightened around the strange doll in her pocket. The coarse hessian rasped her skin. She gripped it tighter and tighter until her knuckles ached and the sudden rush of pain broke her paralysis.

The determination to protect the old lady sent a shock of courage coursing through her veins. With a fearful shriek, Mary rushed towards the malevolent spirit in grey, fighting her way through the mass of hysterical reporters.

When she broke free from the mêlée, she saw the Grey Lady floating away, disappearing along the corridor. Mary chased after the spirit, following it through several rooms, the Grey Lady always just ahead and moving swiftly along. Soon the riot of noise was left behind and Mary was lost, running down wide, echoing passages, past ancient figures and ghostly mythical animals. Even though terror gripped her, her blood was up and she ran faster, determined to catch the spirit.

The wild chase took Mary down one corridor after another, through doors and darkened passages. The spirit, shimmering like liquid, floated in the air, laughing at the desperate maid. Mary followed doggedly.

'She's leading me away!' The thought crashed into Mary's mind like a blow from a hammer. Fortune's protective doll was being lured away from her mistress, so that the centuries-old corpse, rising from the coffin, was free to kill her.

She stopped abruptly, lost in the underground maze and spun around. The Grey Lady stood in front of her, watching her through hollow eyes. Mary's heart pounded.

'Please, leave her alone,' Mary pleaded. 'It's not her fault.' But her voice sounded as if it came from far away, as if it did not belong to her.

'I will have my revenge,' the Grey Lady announced.

Mary reached out, wanting to grab the spirit and shake it into reason.

'But you don't understand—' Something pounded her chest. She flew back, reeling against the wall, and fell down, the wind knocked out of her. The spirit hovered just above her. In the half-light, Mary saw the vacant eyes of the skull, deep recesses of emptiness gazing down at her. The face was a blank. The Grey Lady had no nose, no mouth, no chin.

To Mary's horror, she saw the demon raise its hand. It lifted its veil and began to peel back the bones of its face. A scream froze in Mary's throat. The spirit held a palm before its mouth.

'My breath is death,' it whispered.

The Grey Lady blew a scent of violets into Mary's face.

Mary blinked. Her eyes burned. A mist was forming around her that she tried to brush away. She squeezed her eyes tightly shut and gasped for air, letting loose her frozen scream in a long wailing cry. As she reached out to grasp the spirit, the floor rolled like the swell of the ocean and she clung desperately to the wall to stop herself being washed off the small raft of her shoes. Her heart crashed and pounded. She was drowning in the thick, fuggy air. She clawed at the wall, trying to find something solid to hold on to, only for the floor to ripple and rise up and pull her down. The corridor skewed as she slipped and slithered across the liquid ground.

Mary bit her tongue. She felt nothing, but tasted the blood. She was on her back, looking up at the ceiling which spun in lazy wobbly, circles.

How did I get here? she wondered.

A fat, hairy black spider was slipping down a thread of gossamer, a spider with the face of her brother, Danny, twisting round and round, caught by the swirling eddies of the ceiling. She laughed a vague, strange noise as if it were made by someone else. She looked for the person who could have made it.

'Stop hiding!' Mary barked. 'I know you're here.'

She turned slowly and tried to get on to her hands and knees, but her head kept on turning. It turned a complete circle and she was back where she'd started, staring up at the ceiling again. She tried once again. Then she was looking at the floor. She clawed at the wall trying to find some purchase.

The loathsome Master Noah Fortesque was standing in front of her. The son of her first employer, when Mary was just ten-years-old, looked like he was made of hessian. A large blobby doll, he had an upside-down red heart of felt sewn to his chest, and was pouring gallons of dark brown, dirty water on to the floor from a bucket. She frantically started to mop up the liquid.

'Stop it, stop it!' she shouted. 'Nasty, dirty, boy.'

She mopped more quickly, urgently; she must mop it all up otherwise she'd be in trouble—Mrs Fortesque would be angry and slap her legs and bash her head.

'I'll teach him,' Mary snarled, 'for being such a nasty boy, pulling my hair, dirtying the floor, laughing at me.' She balled her fists remembering just how much she disliked the spoilt little brat.

As she dragged a cloth across the sodden floor, there came a great crashing. Booming footsteps echoed down the hallway. Again, she was lying on the cold floor looking up at the big black spider. But this time it wore Archie's face.

'Hello, Archie,' she giggled. 'You hold him and I'll thump him.'

'Hold who?' The voice came from another room, dull and distant.

'Noah the nasty… little…' Laughing, she swung her fist through the empty air.

'Mary, it's me, Archie.'

She reached up and touched his face.

'Hello, Archie. Did I get him?' She swung again, giggling. 'Bare-knuckle Jessie bashes the nasty little boy,' she giggled.

'Come on.' She felt strong arms lifting her up and she stood, wobbly, swaying like a rag doll, the floor pitching like the deck of a ship. 'Take a deep breath, come on. Deep breaths. In, out. In, out. Come on.'

Mary took several deep breaths in quick succession. 'You hold him—'

'And you'll thump him, yeah, I know.'

Mary giggled again, swinging her fist.

'Deep breaths. See, I ain't forgotten.' Mary sniggered and breathed in and out in quick succession for a good half a minute. Suddenly, her face darkened, her lips contorted, her eyes bulged. 'Oh, my God!' she gasped.

She swallowed loudly, pushed Archie aside and rushed to a corner. Collapsing on her hand and knees, she vomited with deep, guttural groans. Her spasms caught in her throat, her stomach heaved and she spat out the acrid bile. Strings of saliva hung from her lips into the porridge-like mess.

Slowly, Mary turned round and rested against the wall. The sticky drool running from her open mouth, she gazed along the receding corridor with wide eyes. Her face felt bloodless and she gulped her breaths as if she could not get enough air into her lungs.

For several minutes, Mary sat quietly, hearing her breathing, feeling the beating of her heart, aware of the sensation returning to her body; the pain of her bitten tongue, the ache in her head. She felt Archie dabbing her face with a handkerchief and realised he was mopping the spew from around her mouth. She reached out and gingerly touched his cheek to see if he was real.

'If I didn't know better,' he said, 'I'd have said you was drunk.'

'Oh! My head!' Mary groaned loudly. The memory flooded back and she looked up suddenly. The corridor was empty of Grey Ladies, spiders, Fortesques, or water ready to drown her. The ground felt solid, but every so often, it became liquid and she pitched and swayed, despite being seated. 'What happened?'

'You tell me,' Archie said.

Mary clutched him tightly, remembering how the mummy rose from the coffin.

'Did you see…' she garbled her words, unable to make sense of her vision.

'I don't know what I saw,' he said. 'But there was a riot up there. God knows what the press will make of it in tomorrow's papers. Especially if they saw what I thought I saw. That thing climbed out of its coffin. I swear it. And now it's back in its box again, like nothing happened.'

'That's what I… Wait! I saw her!' Mary grasped Archie's arm. Remembering, she tried to rise, but her body felt heavy and awkward. 'The Grey Lady. I saw her. I was chasing her.'

'You did what?'

'She did something to me. Blew her breath in my face, and… and…' Mary slumped back against the wall. '"*My breath is death,*" she said. And… and… her face, Archie.' Fear closed her eyes and she recoiled in horror. 'Her face. It was like a skull, empty sockets where her eyes should have been—but they gleamed as well. I've never seen anything like that before. She had no face, just those eyes… but then I saw a mouth.' She shook her head, not understanding. 'She peeled back the bones of her skull and… and… she had a mouth, as if she was all inside out.'

'All right, all right, tell me later,' Archie said.

Mary raised her hand to wipe her forehead and looked puzzled at the dirty grey rag that was black on one side she was clutching, the edges torn as if it had been ripped away. She remembered. She had been mopping the floor with it. In her other hand, she was clutching Fortune's doll. She had squeezed the doll so hard, it was bent and distorted. The wooden frame was snapped, the stitching popped and the stuffing was hanging out.

'Bloody hell,' Mary said. 'Fortune said it would protect me. I'm still alive, aren't I?'

'And twice as pretty, even with the drool.' He smiled and wiped her face again, looking into Mary's stinging eyes. Her pupils, as wide as pennies, dark and deep, pulsating rhythmically, were reflected in his. 'Though you look like death warmed up.'

'Mrs Grady!' Mary shouted.

❧ 14 ❧

THE AFTERMATH

THEY FOUND Mrs Grady in the room with the sarcophagus. She was seated, almost slumped, and Dr Watson was taking her pulse. The old lady looked strained as if she had aged. Worry creased her pale face, her agitated eyes flicked evasively. A kind of palsy seized her and tremors racked her body. Her fingers fidgeted clutching the crucifix given to her by Mrs Denbie.

'You must rest, Mrs Grady,' Dr Watson was saying. 'You have had a shock—several shocks in the last while. The only cure is rest. I can prescribe some sedatives, but only for the short term. Rest is what you need; otherwise, you will have a breakdown. It is inevitable.'

Mrs Grady nodded absentmindedly and Dr Watson shook his head in frustration.

Mary tentatively approached the sarcophagus and placed a trembling palm against the cold stone, almost expecting to feel the thrumming of life within. Instead, it felt cool and inert, no more alive than the marble statues surrounding them. The brown-stained bandaged body lay perfectly still, the Eye of Horus amulet hung undisturbed on its neck. Nevertheless, a shiver ran up Mary's spine. A vision raced past her eyes of how it had arisen and she quickly looked away.

Some time must have passed since she went chasing after the spirit, but it came as a surprise to learn that an hour had vanished in what appeared to be no more than a few minutes. Archie must have been sitting with her for some while until she regained her reason. Now that the press had departed, the room felt empty.

Dr Watson came over, placed a hand across Mary's forehead and took her pulse. He gazed into her eyes, but shared nothing other than his concerns about Mrs Grady.

'Your mistress has heard me, Mary,' he said, 'but she has not comprehended my advice. Mrs Grady must spend the next week in bed—a week at least. She has been over-worried and her nerves are shredded. I cannot stress this enough: she will have a breakdown unless she takes time to recover away from all that is troubling her.'

'She seemed all right this morning, Dr Watson,' Mary said.

'Her mood will be up and down. It is often the case before the worst happens. But a crisis is coming if she is not careful.'

'A strange business, Dr Watson,' came a voice from

behind them. Mary and the doctor turned to see the dark eyes of Inspector Lestrade. Edging forward, a notebook in his hand, scribbling some words, he gave Mary a polite nod.

'What do you make of it?' he asked the doctor.

'Mass hysteria?' Dr Watson shrugged. 'I have never seen anything like it before. But I remember reading about a case in one of the medical journals where a whole town's inhabitants claimed to have seen ghosts and spirits. The article suggested some common cause.' He nodded to the coffin. 'Like a story from a Penny Dreadful, is it not, Inspector? Walking mummies?'

Lestrade leant over the edge of the sarcophagus and a smile rippled his sallow face.

'This one hasn't walked for three thousand years, Doctor. Not since savages roamed the green plains of England. What do you make of this?' He produced a small doll wrapped in hessian. An upside-down red heart was sewn to its chest. Mary felt for the one she had in her pocket. 'I found it next to Mrs Grady. Dropped out of her bag, I daresay.'

He handed it over. Dr Watson contemplated it for a few seconds and shook his head.

'Voodoo,' was Lestrade's pronouncement. 'We had a case last year. Some poor fellow from the West Indies fell stone dead from heart failure when he was given something like this. It was most peculiar. Only that one had pins stuck into it.'

'Mrs Grady had it?' the Doctor asked and Lestrade nodded.

Archie caught Mary's eyes and flicked his head to where Fortune Dubois was cowering in a shadowy corner.

'Well, thankfully Mrs Grady is still alive,' Dr Watson said, handing the doll back.

'Unlike her colleagues who went on the expedition,' Lestrade said. 'All dead, I read.'

'Most unfortunate series of accidents and events.'

'No doubt your Mr Holmes would see criminals and wrongdoings.'

Dr Watson smiled politely. 'Who knows what Holmes would see?'

'Well, there seems to be no harm done or any crime committed that I am aware of—and I can't very well arrest *this* lady.' He nodded at the mummy and stood beside it with his hands on his hips. 'I shall let you go back to your research, Dr Watson—it is a blessing you were nearby—and make my report as best as I can. But I can't very well write a report concerning Voodoo.'

He gave a small laugh and handed the doll to Mary. 'Miss Finch.' Lestrade tipped his hat good-naturedly. 'It is good to see you have recovered from when last I saw you, after you went for a dip in the Thames.'

'But what about the Grey Lady?' Mary blurted.

'Grey Lady?' Lestrade said.

'I-I-I...' Mary stuttered.

'Oh! I suspect she is suffering from nothing more than the same hysteria everyone else experienced,' Dr Watson interrupted calmly. 'It was pleasant to meet you again, Inspector. I shall give your good regards to Mr Holmes.'

Lestrade smiled appreciatively. 'I only wish I had been here to see the apparition. I could have dined out on it for a good while, I suspect,' and he wandered away.

'I am sorry to have cut you short, Mary,' Dr Watson said. 'But along with everything else, it is best if Lestrade does not upset Mrs Grady with yet more questions about things she cannot explain. She has much on her mind?'

Mary did not answer, not wishing to share her mistress's troubles, merely thanking Dr Watson for all his efforts on Mrs Grady's behalf.

'Now remember, she must rest and do nothing stressful,' the doctor said. 'This is a sleeping draught for tonight only. The signs point to a breakdown and it will not take much to push her over the edge. Have her doctor drop by, I am sure he will confirm my diagnosis.'

After he left, Mary drifted over to where Fortune was hiding, leaving Archie to look after Mrs Grady. She was surprised Fortune was there and not safely at school as she should have been. Seeing how frightened the girl seemed, sitting with her legs drawn up and her arms around them, rather than berating her, Mary eased down beside her. She showed Fortune the second doll.

'I made it for Mistress,' Fortune admitted. She sucked her lips and clucked noisily in annoyance. 'Me knew something bad would happen if she come here and it would protect her.'

'Did you give her it?'

Fortune shook her head. 'No, Miss Mary, Miss Ella slip it into her bag without she knowing.'

'Ella? Little scallywags!' Mary mumbled under her breath. 'How did you get here?' she asked.

'I walked,' Fortune said matter-of-factly. Mary gave a small, surprised laugh. The scullery maid walked four miles to look after her employer without a second thought. Mary would need to think twice before calling Fortune ungrateful again. She wondered how Fortune even found her way.

'Did you see what happened?' Mary asked.

Fortune shook her head. 'I was hiding when I heard all the noise. I got scared.' Her eyes dropped and she looked at her feet.

'So, you didn't see anything.'

'I saw she, the Grey Lady,' Fortune said and Mary leaned closer. 'She was running away.'

'Running? Not floating? Flying?' Mary remembered how the spirit floated in front of her, always just out of reach.

Fortune gave her an odd look. 'No, Miss Mary, she was running. I chased after she like you did, but I couldn't keep up with you. I got lost, and then she ran past me and into a room, and…' Fortune's eyes lowered in confusion. 'She vanished, Miss Mary. There was only another lady in the room, in a black dress. She must have seen the Grey Lady. There was only one door to the room, so the Grey Lady must have…' Fortune shrugged, '…vanished.'

The girl looked at the doll. 'Am I in trouble, Miss Mary? Will Mistress be angry at me? Cook will. She'll beat me.'

Mary smiled, knowing Cook was all bluster. Although she would not care to admit it, Cook secretly liked Fortune.

'Listen, let's make a pact. I won't tell Mrs Grady about this if you won't. Not that I think she'd be angry. But just so Cook doesn't find out. And I'm ever so grateful for your doll. It got a bit damaged, I'm afraid.' She showed Fortune the battered doll. 'But I swear it protected me from that evil thing.'

'Jumbies are afraid of the light and the goodness inside the dolls,' Fortune said proudly. 'Not all dolls are evil, Miss Mary. Not that that policeman knows anything.' She pouted and gave Inspector Lestrade an evil stare. 'Or he'd have investigated—'

'You've seen him before? Inspector Lestrade?'

Fortune nodded.

'Was it that case he spoke about when you saw him? The man who was given the doll and died?'

Fortune was silent.

'Was that your dad, Fortune?'

The small girl leant over, buried her head against Mary's shoulder and sobbed quietly. Mary wrapped her arms around her and held her tightly.

THE REPORT ONLY MADE PAGE THREE OF THE *DAILY Telegraph*. Even so, the headlines glared.

THE PRIESTESS NEFRUSHERI RISES FROM HER COFFIN

THE CURSE OF ANCIENT EGYPT COMES TO THE BRITISH MUSEUM

A GHOST IN THE BRITISH MUSEUM

Absurd as it may seem in this day and age to describe the doings of a ghost, we feel it is our duty as journalists not to leave unrecorded events which occurred yesterday at the British Museum, Bloomsbury. The events we are about to describe can be well authenticated as they were witnessed by a dozen members of the press.

On Friday noontime, on the occasion of the opening of the sarcophagus belonging to the high priestess Nefrusheri, the following occurred.

As the lid to the casket was raised, we became aware of a spectral being rising from the depths of the coffin. At first, we thought we were being deceived, a trick of the light caused by the glare of the many camera flash trays there to record the event. But the presence of the shadowy being was seemingly beyond dispute

At that same moment, another ghostly figure was

observed. A skeletal lady dressed entirely in grey was seen to hover in mid-air behind the members of the press.

Yet in no more than a few minutes, it became clear that what we had seen was a visual hallucination, the cause of which was explained by Mr Julian Barclay, Curator of Egyptian Antiquities at the British Museum, to be due to the inhalation of the foul air that had been trapped inside the sarcophagus. Once released, it affected all present with ghostly imaginings.

The affair has caused much excitement, as this sarcophagus was an artefact returned from the expedition sponsored by Mrs Jane Rose Grady of Holland Park. Following said enterprise, several unfortunate deaths have occurred, believed to be the result of a curse placed by Nefrusheri to guard her tomb.

A PHOTOGRAPH ACCOMPANIED THE ARTICLE. IT SHOWED the casket containing the mummy, the lid suspended above and to one side. Beyond it, Mrs Grady, Mr Barclay and others stood with petrified looks on their faces. Reflected in a polished mirror behind them was the Grey Lady.

15

MR FOGARTY HAWTHORNE
CALLS

THAT SATURDAY the household awoke to a riot of
newspapermen. They were anxious for a story of the
mummy's curse, how Nefrusheri wreaked her vengeance
on those who'd dared defile her last resting place. Added
to them came a stream of mediums and clairvoyants,
none of whom believed Mr Barclay's explanation of bad
air, all quite prepared to free the old lady from the atten-
tions of a wicked spirit at only a *slight* cost for their
troubles.

Mary read the news report and a strange sense of
foreboding came back to her. As she sat staring at
Fortune's doll, the images from the previous day played
through her mind—the mummy rising from the casket;
the Grey Lady blowing her foetid breath into her face;
how the world spun afterwards, waking inherent fears of
drowning within her. When she closed her eyes, she

could clearly see the skull-like head and the way the Grey Lady seemed to peel back its bones to reveal lips and a mouth.

Her worries for Mrs Grady increased considerably. The lady had aged since yesterday. She refused the advice of both her own doctor and Dr Watson to stay in bed. Her bedroom was too claustrophobic, she complained, and she would not be persuaded to rest there. Instead, like a lost spirit, she haunted the morning room. Pale, vacant, prone to fits of trembling, she picked at her breakfast. Her mind was clearly disturbed, and there was little Mary could do but watch. As Dr Watson predicted, she was teetering on the edge of a breakdown.

Once again, the doorbell sounded as it had done so often that morning. Expecting yet more newspapermen or spiritual helpers, Mary watched as Mr Venables admitted on this occasion a dour elderly man, dressed in mourning black. Tall and ruddy-cheeked, with dark empty eyes, his nose beak-like, he wore a serpentine smile, made more so by his flicking tongue that constantly licked his lips. His business card named him as Mr Fogarty Hawthorne, a solicitor with offices in Greek Street, Soho.

'If it's anything to do with yesterday—' Mr Venables started to say, but the visitor quietly shook his head.

'No, nothing at all to do with spirits. Ghosts, perhaps; spirits, no,' he said enigmatically.

Despite Mary and Mr Venables's misgivings, Mrs

Grady agreed to see him. However, she asked Mary to remain with them should she need anything.

'She's had a shock,' Mary warned the solicitor before they went into the morning room. 'You ain't gonna upset her, are you? I know what you *snipes* are like.'

'Ah!' the solicitor said, and smiled politely at the description of his profession. 'That I can't guarantee.'

Mary thought him a thoroughly disagreeable man.

Mr Hawthorne sat rigidly in a chair and scanned the room idly and quietly, as if waiting for the maid to leave. But Mary planted herself firmly behind the old lady. She rested a hand on Mrs Grady's shoulder, silently announcing her intention to remain. When Mrs Grady did not dismiss her, Mr Hawthorne smiled his serpentine smile and dug inside his briefcase, removing a number of documents.

'I'm afraid my business might be upsetting,' he apologised. 'So, I think it appropriate to get straight to the point.'

Mrs Grady nodded. He took a deep breath.

'Madam, I represent Mrs Siobhan Cara Grady, née Fitzwilliam,' he said firmly.

A judder ran through Mrs Grady and she swayed. Mary, who only recently heard that name, and then in such peculiar circumstances, was worried to hear it again so soon.

'My husband's first wife?' Mrs Grady asked quietly. 'I-I don't understand.'

Mr Hawthorne's eyes fixed the old lady with a curious stare.

'Perhaps we could have some tea,' he said, 'and then, Mrs Grady, we can discuss this more.'

Mary huffed. She wanted to ask when did guests start ordering tea, but Mrs Grady made a slight nod to indicate that she should obey. Mary, though, only went as far as the communications' cord to the kitchen and gave it a pull before coming back. She saw the disappointment in Mr Hawthorne's face that she was going to stay.

When Fortune came, Mary ordered tea. Looking at the solicitor, she added, 'Better bring some biscuits as well, in case he gets peckish,' and resumed her guard behind her mistress.

'Perhaps you can explain yourself,' Mrs Grady said croakily.

'Well now, where shall we start?' Mr Hawthorne smiled again. Mary did not much care for that odd smile —it was as if he was enjoying himself, taking pleasure in Mrs Grady's discomfort. Nor did she much care for the deliberate way he did everything, like unfolding pieces of paper to show Mrs Grady. And each time he smiled, her sense of foreboding increased.

'This is a copy of the marriage certificate of Patrick Liam Grady to Miss Siobhan Cara Fitzwilliam,' he said. 'They were joined in Castlemaine. It is dated 1847. The lady was seventeen when—'

'I know of this, Mr Hawthorne,' Mrs Grady said.

He nodded politely. 'The marriage took place during the awful famine that affected Ireland—'

'I know of the famine, Mr Hawthorne, I was there,' Mrs Grady said.

'Of course. Pardon me. By all accounts, Patrick was something of a rogue—'

'And I also know of my husband's past, sir.'

'I dare say.' Mr Hawthorne coughed. He steepled his fingers together and sat back, resting his hands on his stomach. 'Then you may also know that the marriage was frowned upon, and Siobhan was disowned by her family. Not long after the marriage, Patrick Grady was arrested for robbery and sentenced to several years in prison. Devoid of her husband's support as well as her family, Siobhan fell into a state of melancholy—a condition she had been prone to all her life. By all accounts, she lost her sanity.

'The why is of no importance, but fearful for her wellbeing, her family arranged a reconciliation. The terms were to be her divorce from Patrick Grady on some technicality. But by then, the famine took its toll on her family too and matters were left unfinished.'

Mary felt the old lady's tremors and clutched her shoulder more tightly.

'What's all this got to do with Mrs Grady?' she asked sharply.

Mr Hawthorne's reptilian smile returned.

'Siobhan found herself alone once more. Needless to

say, by then she had become devoid of reason. One might have called her a lunatic, as she displayed such tendencies. In a fit of depression, she attempted to take her life.'

The solicitor quietly waited, taking his time before continuing.

'On his release from prison, Patrick Grady found a broken woman, constantly at war with herself, a moment away from the completion of that mortal sin. Most of her close family succumbed to the famine, as had her child, or they fled the country; she was alone. No doubt feeling responsible for her, Patrick committed her to an asylum in Dublin as the only charitable thing he could do. He had money—proceeds of another robbery, I believe—and paid for her life-long incarceration, and she resides there… to this day.'

Mrs Grady flinched.

'To this—? No, that is not true,' she said. 'Siobhan is dead. She was buried in the cemetery of St Anne's soon after Patrick's release from prison. Her grave was shown to me by my husband.'

'I beg to differ, Mrs Grady.' Hawthorne dropped his gaze and looked at her from under his brow, and didn't bother hide the smirk he wore. In a calm, restrained voice, he continued. 'Siobhan Grady was placed in the tender care of the sisters of mercy, in whose company she has resided for over forty years.'

The old lady wiped a handkerchief across her forehead; then she wrung her hands and sat uneasily.

'She survived, madam, I assure you,' Mr Hawthorne said. He reached inside his briefcase and withdrew a document that he placed on the table. 'This is a testament from the good sisters as to her status. It speaks of her condition as being healthy and no longer prone to malignant thoughts of suicide.'

A shaky hand attested to Mr Hawthorne's story. These were the last words written by Sister Joan of St Anselm's asylum for the insane, who, Mr Hawthorne said, recently and sadly passed away.

'It was only when Sister Joan read about the Egyptian expedition, that she realised who you were and that Patrick Grady had died. It was she who informed Siobhan. Her testament is legal,' he added.

The old lady's skin turned icy. Mary heard Lorna Denbie's voice echoing in her head.

'*Siobhan—she who had gone before you, who was lost but still is.*'

She wondered if the old lady was hearing that same voice as well.

'I-I don't understand,' Mrs Grady stuttered. 'But… but… she must come and live here, with me… Siobhan must come… Mary, she must come…' Mrs Grady mumbled, then she fell silent.

Some minutes passed and the odd smile, which never seemed to leave the solicitor's lips, grew wider. He slowly sat upright, fixing Mrs Grady with his eyes.

'Madam,' he said gravely, 'I am a messenger of ill

news. My business at times necessitates such disturbing communications, in which I take no great pleasure. Yet I must discharge my duties faithfully.'

He took a deep breath. 'It has long been assumed that Patrick Grady died intestate—that is, he left no will or testament. And his estate passed to you as his supposedly lawful wife, since he apparently had no other relatives.'

'Supposedly lawful?' Mary said. 'What do you mean?'

'However, that is not the case,' Mr Hawthorne continued, ignoring the maid. 'As his first wife lives, madam, and there is no record of a separation, it is my sorry duty to inform you that your marriage to Patrick Grady is invalid. Furthermore, he did make a will soon after his marriage to Siobhan Fitzwilliam, which he left in her care. The will was never revoked. I have it here,' he patted his briefcase.

'What's that mean?' Mary asked.

'It means,' Mr Hawthorne said, 'that Siobhan Cara Grady, née Fitzwilliam, is the single true beneficiary of Patrick Grady's estate. She is willing to go to a court of law to claim her entitlement.'

Mrs Grady stiffened before a shudder racked her body. She struggled to breathe. Mr Hawthorne continued relentlessly.

'Madam, while you may be due some compensation for the fact that the estate has prospered since his death,' he said as a by-the-by, 'Patrick Grady's estate, and all that it has become in the ensuing years, lawfully belongs to Siobhan Grady.'

'But that can't be right,' Mary said.

'Right or wrong, it is legal.' Mr Hawthorne shrugged and stared back with an amused expression.

Mrs Grady sat in silence for several minutes. When she finally moved, Mary could sense the effort it took her to lift a shaky hand towards the lawyer. It was Mr Hawthorne's turn to look confused as he perceived that the interview was over. He gathered up his papers with some annoyance at the lack of reaction to his shocking announcement, ignored the proffered hand, and quickly left.

When he reached the front door, he turned to Mary.

'Tell your mistress, this is not over,' he said angrily.

Mary hurried back to find Mrs Grady sitting mumbling quietly to herself. The old lady's eyes stared ahead and saw nothing.

16

COOK AND MR VENABLES ARGUE

SOMETHING DIED in Mrs Grady that day. She was no longer the splendid woman, happy and eternally young, the subject of the beautiful painting that hung in the downstairs drawing room. Now she sat, collapsed and broken and racked with doubt, shying away from those around her, much to Mary's consternation.

The doctor was sent for immediately, and Mrs Grady was put to bed. She wore a faraway look: vacant and afraid like a lost child. She mumbled constantly, fidgeting incessantly with the cross given to her, and Mary feared Dr Watson's pronouncement was coming true. So many things had happened to the old lady in such a short time, Mary wondered how she would cope.

When the doctor left, the house felt as if it was in mourning. A sombre quiet closeted each room. That was, until Mary told Cook and Mr Venables what happened with the solicitor. Then an argument began.

'No!' Cook shouted. 'Siobhan Fitzwilliam died during the famine.'

'But did you see the body?' Mr Venables asked.

'I did not. But she was as near to death as anyone could be when last I saw her. If she's not dead, then who is buried at St Anne's?'

'I do not know. My business took me elsewhere at the time,' Mr Venables said. 'I cannot swear to what happened afterwards.'

'I *can* because *I* was there,' Cook said firmly. She grasped the Butler's arm. 'Tobias, Patrick Grady looked a haunted man when I saw him and I will swear it was because of Siobhan's death. He was going to Dublin to take ship for England. I said I'd accompany him as I had family in need of me there. He refused my offer, saying he would not be good company on any journey. But I swear, Tobias, he left by himself. He took no one with him. I will swear to it!'

'Even so, you can't be sure that he didn't take Siobhan to Dublin with him, can you?'

'She passed away by then,' Cook said adamantly.

'But you did not see her body!' Mr Venables pounded the table. 'Were you at her funeral? No! It was a private affair with but a single mourner and an unmarked grave, the stone yet to be purchased. He may well have lied for whatever reason and taken her to Dublin with him, for all we know.'

'But to place Siobhan in a lunatic asylum and forget about her?' Cook said. 'That is not the man I knew.'

Mr Venables huffed and Cook grabbed his arm once more.

'He would not have just left her there to rot. And when he met Rosie, he would have told her about Siobhan, not lied and taken her to another's grave—to prove what?'

Mr Venables pulled away to stand by himself.

'Patrick was a lot of things, Tobias, and he's burning in hell for many of them, I'm sure, but not for doing that foul deed. You knew the man as well as I.'

'Yes, Eileen, and better than most.' He gave a deep scowl.

'And what do you mean by that?' Cook asked.

'You didn't know Patrick as well as I. You didn't know what he was capable of. There are many things you do not know about him.'

'What are you saying? Come, man, out with it.'

Mr Venables swallowed. "Have you considered whether Patrick did divorce Siobhan? Because if he did not, and she is living…'

Cook looked at Mr Venables, aghast. An angry flush lit her face and she sat down and stared dumbly at the table. Mr Venables, reluctant to say more, fell quiet.

In the short time Mary knew them, she had never seen Cook and Mr Venables argue like this. She knew they had all grown up together—Mr Venables, Cook, Mrs Grady and Patrick—and their friendship ran deep. She was confused, not only by what Cook and Mr Venables spoke of, but also what Mr Hawthorne said. Mary's eyes wandered along the corridor and to the stairs, to the room where Mrs Grady slept.

'Just what does all that stuff about wills mean, Mr Venables?' she asked, not willing to discuss the possibility that Patrick and Siobhan were never separated.

The Butler composed himself. His face was grim.

'*If* it is true,' he said, '*if* Siobhan is alive and there is a will that states she is the only heir, and *if* there are no later wills, then all of this—' he threw up his hand to indicate the whole house— 'is hers. None of it is Rosie's.'

He sat down heavily.

'And *if* she and Patrick were never divorced…' he looked over and saw the pain in Cook's face, '… then all of this is her entitlement, regardless of wills.'

'Mrs Grady will have to leave?' Mary asked. 'She'll lose it all?'

'Aye, girl. Everything. Patrick did not leave Rosie a will. We searched when we heard of his death, but one was never found. Perhaps he took it to the grave with him. Now she will be dependent on Siobhan Grady's charity and the meagre amount the law will give her for… for what? For being the caretaker of his estate? And that may be little indeed.'

'Forty odd years!' Cook said softly through her tears. 'In all that time, was Siobhan so content in that asylum that she had no curiosity about what happened to Patrick? Or why he never came back for her? And poor Rosie will be ridiculed, Tobias.'

'Patrick Grady, what a merry chase you have led us,' Mr Venables said angrily.

That evening, Mary sat in bed and worried for her mistress. The dreadful news of Patrick Grady's will had arrived to heap itself on top of everything else that had happened to the old lady—the threats to her life; the reminders of her husband's awful deeds; the deaths of her friend and his companions in mysterious circumstances; the dreadful curse and the terrible events at the museum. All these things sat on Mrs Grady like a crushing weight.

'This on top of everything else.' Mary stroked the cat.

Oscar looked up through bleary eyes, for once seeming attentive. Whatever it was that affected him on the day of the séance seemed to have passed. For several days afterwards, however, he walked almost drunkenly.

'That girl predicted it as well. She knew all about Patrick, about Mrs Grady, about Siobhan. Why would she have mentioned her name otherwise? "*I heard a voice cry Siobhan*", wasn't that what she said? She knows about Danny as well. I'm worried, Oz.'

Mary held the single photograph she owned of her

family, traced a finger across the faces and shook her head slowly. Lorna Denbie had been right all the time. What terrible ghosts were raised.

'I can't leave her alone, Oz. I was going to go to Camden Town to find Mrs Fortesque tomorrow. But I can't leave Mrs Grady in the state she's in, especially if that snake of a snipe comes back. He was enjoying himself, Oz. He can't *guarantee* he's not gonna upset her! You could have fooled me. Ordering *tea* like he owned the place! *Smiling* all the time!' She scowled.

As she blew out the candle, her sense of unease returned.

17

A GHOSTLY INTRUDER

THAT NIGHT, Mary dreamt of the sea and rivers. Of drowning. Of her father and mother underwater. Of her brother, Danny Finch, lost and asking for help. And again, her dreams woke her well before dawn.

The wind and rain were beating against the window. The house, though, rested like an empty church. She lay back and listened to the noises outside and the quietness inside, but her mind, like the weather, could not and would not be stilled. The revelations of the previous day demanded to be heard again and again and again and would not give her peace.

She threw back the blankets in frustration. She was covered in sweat. As she sat up in bed, odd worries gnawed at her. She lit the oil lamp, found a book on the bedside table and began reading. Reaching down, she stroked the silky fur of Oscar, but after half an hour of reading, she was aware that she could not recall a single sentence. The engine that was her mind would not switch itself off and ran its journey elsewhere, not in her book.

She gazed around the room, at the strange shadows cast by the lamp, at the cracked ceiling and the cold gleam on the mirror. Outside, it had stopped raining. She closed her eyes in frustration and saw only ghosts.

Then her heart missed a beat.

Oscar was crouching beside the door. The cat had leapt silently off the bed. Every hair on his body stood on end, his ears were erect, his whiskers drawn back, his body was tensed. A soft, low growl came from the back of his throat, followed by an urgent spitting hiss.

Mary sat up, paralysed with fear. She listened intently. The house was silent but for the beating of her heart and the cat snuffling at the door, scratching at it, pulling it back an inch or two. With another hiss, he eased out of the room in a low crouch.

Mary climbed out of bed, grasped the fireside poker and followed the cat. Oscar vanished into the gloom of the corridor. She went further down the passageway, hardly breathing, and began to descend the stairs from her attic room, the light coming through her open door illuminating the path. The treads creaked loudly and she flinched and listened nervously. Not a sound. She raised the poker high and continued.

She stepped off the last tread and gazed down the long passageway. Ahead in the darkness, she could hear the guttural hiss of the cat. He was crouching beside Mrs Grady's room, pawing at the door, scratching it with his claws, trying to pull it open, getting more and more agitated, snarling and hissing, back arched.

A cold breeze was blowing along the passageway, making Mary shiver. To her surprise, Mary saw Fortune and Ella stealthily climbing the stairs, holding each other's hands, crouched and tensed like the cat. Their eyes were fixed on Mrs Grady's door. The cold breeze, running up the stairs, fluttered their nightdresses.

Before Mary could speak, a hideous scream shattered the silence, coming from Mrs Grady's room. As Mary rushed forward and grasped the door handle, she heard Fortune and Ella's frightened cries.

She pushed against the door. Something crashed into her and threw her back out of the room. She collided with the opposite side of the corridor with a thump, her head banging against the wall. There was a vague impression of a grey shape sweeping past and racing away. All sense of time seemed to vanish in an instant.

Ella's piercing cries brought her back to her senses and she stumbled into Mrs Grady's room. Mary was aware that lights were going on and the clatter of foot-steps, seemingly from every direction, were converging on the bedroom. Ella was screaming at Mrs Grady to wake up, frantically pulling her arm. The old woman lay half in and half out of bed. Mr Venables arrived and pushed Ella aside, immediately grasping the old lady's wrist, feeling for a pulse.

In Mary's daze, time was passing oddly. Her head was sore and she rubbed it. The strange mist she'd seen in the basement of the British Museum hung in front of her eyes. She was aware that Cook was seated beside Mrs Grady. Her mistress was propped upright in bed, slumped over, her eyes closed.

'How much did you take?' Cook was shouting. 'Rosie, how much?' She gave Mrs Grady several sharp slaps across the face as she demanded an answer, holding a bottle of laudanum, waving it in front of Mrs Grady's vacant eyes. 'Tell me,' Cook shouted.

'Damn it, Eileen, where'd she get this from?' Mr Venables said. 'Wake up, Rosie,' and he shook her. 'Get her up! Make her walk. Don't let her fall asleep. I'll get the doctor.'

'You try dying on me, Rose Grady, and I swear I'll never forgive you,' Cook shouted through her tears. 'I swear I'll not bring a single flower to your grave. You'll be buried in unconsecrated ground and no one will ever come and see you.'

Cook was dragging Mrs Grady to her feet, pulling her along. The mistress moved mechanically, limply and dumbly with her.

'Walk for my sake, Rosie.' Cook forced back her tears. 'Please. Walk, Rosie.'

Mary blinked away her own tears, trying to bring

herself back to the present. She felt a bump rising on her head where it met the wall. She recalled Oscar's strange behaviour, Ella and Fortune in front of her, the thing that struck her, the grey figure moving past. Then a shock racked her body. She rushed to the door, glanced along the passageway and rushed back inside Mrs Grady's room again, grasping Ella firmly by the wrist.

'Where's Fortune?' Mary said, shaking Ella who gazed up in abject terror. 'Where's Fortune?' she demanded again.

'She chased after her,' Ella stuttered.

'Chased after who?' Mary shouted.

'The Grey Lady! The Grey Lady!' Ella screamed, trying to get away from the angry maid. 'Leave me alone, you're hurting me,' she cried.

Mary realised how hard she was shaking the girl while still holding a poker in her hand.

❧ 18 ❧

THE SEARCH FOR FORTUNE DUBOIS

MARY DRESSED QUICKLY and hurried out of the house to search for Fortune. There was little she could do to help Mrs Grady. Even when the doctor arrived, she would be of no real use.

She felt groggy from banging her head against the wall, but concerns for the small girl made her ignore Cook's advice. Waiting for the doctor would take too long. Enough of the fog cleared from her mind for her to remember the rushing grey figure leaving Mrs Grady's room. How much time passed since then, she could not say. But enough for Fortune to have gone chasing after a spirit.

The French window to the drawing room was wide open. That was the source of the cold breeze she'd felt when she'd tiptoed down from her attic room. Someone must have entered the house through it. Mary noticed muddy footprints extending from the garden and across the carpet.

Was it here the Grey Lady entered the house? She rubbed her head to ease the throb of the bump, paused in confusion and knelt beside the marks. Mary gazed to see where they'd come from. There were three sets of footprints in the wet grass. One set, the same size as the ones on the drawing room floor, led to another set, going away from the house and across the lawn. Next to them was a smaller set of prints.

The grass, wet from the recent rain, was trampled in a long, broken line, making a clear path for her to follow. It led across the lawn, past a screen of trees and over a piece of open ground to the high wall that surrounded the property. She climbed the wall and eased down the other side into Holland Park.

After a dozen paces, the path in the crushed grass vanished at a gritty black cinder track. Seeing that the trampled grass was leading to the left, she continued in that direction. She shouted Fortune's name. There came no reply.

The cinder track led to a gate in a low wall. The gate was padlocked, but a patch of wet grass beside it was trampled almost flat. She climbed the wall and eased herself down onto a pavement outside the park. The trail disappeared.

She stood quietly and scanned left and right along the road. Rows of dark houses stretched away in both directions. Which way would they have gone? She could choose one, but soon she would come to other streets and avenues. Fortune could have taken any one of them in pursuit of the Grey Lady. Before long, the permutations would be countless.

She stood and listened, hoping to hear the clatter of footsteps to suggest a direction to follow. The street was hushed. From somewhere behind the houses, a dog barked. Birds were singing in the park, greeting the dawn. Wind rustled the leaves. But there were no other sounds.

Mary ran her fingers through her hair and rubbed her neck. Unable to make up her mind which way to go she felt herself getting warm with frustration. As the knot in her stomach tightened, her thoughts raced.

What got into Fortune? She was a wilful child. Hadn't she walked unbidden all the way to Bloomsbury to look after Mrs Grady? Perhaps she had one of her strange dolls with her and felt safe. Even so, Mary could not help but imagine Fortune lying maybe in a back street, maybe behind some wall, maybe murdered in an abandoned room, all alone, away from the people who loved her. The haunting images consumed the few rational thoughts Mary had, leaving her dejected and afraid.

She shook her head to clear the dreadful visions away and stood, frozen with doubt. Sighing loudly, she felt like she wanted to scream. Her head drooped and she slumped inwards. She could only hope that Fortune was safe, that the young girl had given up the chase and was back home. In despair, uncertain where to look and what to do, Mary sat on the pavement, her feet in the gutter, feeling utterly useless.

'Stop it,' she said after several minutes. 'This ain't doing Fortune any good. She's the one in trouble, not you.' But all she could do was to ease back on to her arms and stare blankly into the sky.

When the hot flushes of frustration subsided, she shivered in the cold morning air. A good hour passed since she began her search and she had achieved nothing.

'Come on, Finch,' she said, 'there ain't no use sitting here. Get up! Come on, get up!' Yet she remained where she was. 'What would Mr Holmes do? Not sit here feeling sorry for himself. He'd think. He'd work out a plan. That's what he'd do, and that's what you need to do. He'd add up all the facts and see what there was. And there's an awful lot of facts to examine now. And you can't do that sitting here!'

She arose wearily.

It would have been quicker to go back the way she had come, retracing her footsteps across Holland Park. But on the off chance of finding something significant, she took the long way home. By the time she arrived at the house, the sky was a pale blue and the sun was starting to rise.

The house was in uproar.

❧ 19 ❧

THE BREAK-IN THAT WASN'T

'What now?' Mary moaned.

Several carriages lined the street. The police entering and leaving the house was to be expected, but Mr Venables and Fogarty Hawthorne facing each other angrily on the front steps was not. Mary rubbed her throbbing head and wondered if it were possible for the day to get any worse.

'I'll not be fobbed off,' Mr Hawthorne shouted. Mr Venables stood in his way, barring him from entering the house.

'Mrs Grady is ill. I'll thank you to keep your voice down and show a little respect,' he said.

'Ill? She was fine when I saw her yesterday. Under the weather, but fine enough. How convenient that she is so ill so suddenly.'

'That was then. Now, if you don't get off, I'll give you such a hiding…' Mr Venables raised his fists.

'Threats? To an officer of the court? Did you hear that?' Hawthorne shouted to the policeman standing in the hallway. 'I'd have you in front of the judge before the blood dries. You just try it and see what happens.'

'It's Sunday, man. Surely your business could have waited a single day.'

'The law does not take Sundays off as the good Inspector will attest.' The solicitor flicked his head towards the inside of the house, where Inspector Lestrade stood watching.

'You'll have to wait, won't you?' Mr Venables said angrily.

'And what's wrong with her, may I ask?' Hawthorne placed his hands on his hips arrogantly. Mary noticed his serpentine smile had returned.

'She's come down with an ailment,' Mr Venables responded. 'Ask the *good* Inspector, if you don't believe me.'

Hawthorne smirked wickedly as if he was taking pleasure from the uproar. At that moment, Cook appeared with folded arms. There was an unconcealed antipathy for the solicitor on her face and he backed down the steps.

'There's some trickery at work here,' he snapped. 'She'll have to face the law and answer for her deeds. You can't shield her, and no lies about her health will save her. She'll need a lawyer, and a good one at that, if she's to keep hold of her possessions. But mark my words well: all of this belongs to my client.' He flung his arms out towards the house. 'Siobhan Grady will have it all. Ghostly grey ladies attacking your mistress will be the least of her worries.'

He threw some papers at Mr Venables and stormed towards the gate. Mary stepped out of his way to avoid a collision. When he passed her, he wheeled around.

'And taking poison won't save her from justice,' he hissed to Mary, and then he was away.

Mary had seen people like him before—driven by greed; brutal people who did not care whom they hurt. She turned to the Butler for an explanation.

'Summons and a writ of intent,' Mr Venables said quietly as he collected the scattered papers. 'She has to appear at a hearing to see if there is merit in the case.'

'Is there merit, Mr Venables?' Mary asked.

The Butler did not answer.

'She's in no condition to go anywhere,' Cook said.

'He means to press the claim no matter what state she's in, Eileen.'

'This will kill her for sure.'

'Grasping man!' Mr Venables swore as he watched Hawthorne climb into his carriage. 'Just turning up out of the blue, expecting to see Rosie,' he shouted at him.

'Did he just turn up, Mr Venables?' Mary asked.

'Not a minute ago. Expecting to come into the house,'

he huffed.

Mary's brows knitted as she watched the carriage pull away. She was puzzled. She stepped inside. The house was busy. Policemen were coming and going and Inspector Lestrade was with Mrs Grady's doctor at the foot of the stairs.

'It was as I suspected, Inspector,' the doctor said. 'According to the Butler, Mrs Grady had been complaining of pains all day, and he administered laudanum to help make her comfortable.' Mary started to protest, but she was ignored. 'It is a poison, of course, and should really be given under medical supervision. But there it is, people will ignore advice. There was a mix-up, I would say. When I asked how much laudanum had been taken, we came to the conclusion of between five and seven teaspoons full, judging by the amount missing from the bottle.'

'Five and seven?' Lestrade said. 'An unusually large amount, doctor?'

The doctor nodded. 'However, there was some uncertainty. Her symptoms, though, were enough to convince me she had been poisoned—her face was haggard, her pupils were closely contracted, suggesting an emetic should be administered. The result was instant and produced full vomiting, which smelled strongly of laudanum. I administered a quart of warm water, and the further copious vomiting that ensued persuaded me that the stomach was completely empty.'

'How did she come to take such a large dose?' Lestrade asked.

'The Butler said she had taken one spoonful before bed. It would have left her drowsy and disorientated, so I suggest she awoke and, believing sufficient time had passed and finding she was still in pain, took another. Then something similar must have happened when she awoke again, when in reality, very little time had elapsed between doses. I have seen this kind of accident all too often. It would have been good practice to have locked the bottle away.'

'So, not suicide?'

'Suicide! Did you not hear what the doctor just said?' Cook shouted. 'The very thought. She's a good church-going woman, Inspector.'

'I merely wondered if the lady has been under any stress.'

'Stress? Rose Grady? Even if she was, she'd never contemplate such a thing. And leaving the bottle there was my fault. It'll not happen again.'

Lestrade made to say something. Cook's po-faced expression disconcerted him. She clearly lied and Mary suspected, he knew that, but rather than saying anything, he gave a slight nod of his head. Seeing Mary, he came towards her, and they walked over to the drawing room.

'A break in as well,' he said. 'It is lucky for your mistress that there was one and it woke everyone, otherwise she would have lain there undisturbed and no doubt have died. Did you see the intruder? And don't go giving me ghost stories, please, Miss Finch, it is far too early in the morning.' He gave a shake of his head and glanced back at Ella, who was watching them with wide, swollen eyes from the top of the stairs.

'I banged my head,' Mary said truthfully. 'I don't know what I saw.'

'Perhaps I can relieve you of that,' the policeman said. Mary realised she was still carrying the poker and her hand was shaking.

'Do you think the little West Indian girl had something to do with it? And ran away?' Lestrade asked.

'Of course not!' Mary snapped. 'She went following her, and I'm worried she's not back. Can't you get you men to search—'

'It is being done as we speak. She went following *her*? What did you mean by *her*?'

'I-I thought the intruder looked like a woman.'

'A woman? All in grey, I suppose.' Again he glanced pursed lipped towards Ella. 'More ghost stories?' he mumbled.

'Look, Inspector, I can only tell you what I know, and if you don't believe it, what's the point of telling you?'

'All right, Miss Finch, I did not mean to raise your hackles,' Lestrade said, smiling. 'But after that affair in the British Museum... do you still believe in this ghost?'

'Since when do ghosts leave footprints?' Mary asked, walking into the drawing room and pointing to the marks on the floor. Inspector Lestrade knelt down to examine them.

'Very observant.' He nodded. 'Small, delicate footprints. Burglary! Breaking and entering is men's work. I suggest a small man rather than a woman—a nimble cat burglar. Nothing is missing, the Butler says. It looks like he was surprised before he had time to take anything. Probably by the little girls. Yes! A professional thief. Came to the back of the house via Holland Park—no doubt to avoid being seen on the road.'

'Why did *she* go upstairs, then?' Mary asked.

'*He* thought there would be better pickings there, I suspect,' Lestrade mused.

Mary looked around at the silver candlestick holders, the ornate cigarette boxes, the expensive ornaments that dotted the room and gave the policeman a caustic look, but said nothing. Instead, she crouched beside the latch of the French windows. It had been forced—the scratches were fresh. She gazed out to the lawn, seeing Fortune's small footprints near the larger ones, and worried about the small girl.

Upstairs, she found Cook seated on Mrs Grady's bed.

'All right,' Mary whispered angrily, not wishing to disturb the sleeping lady. 'I been here long enough to know where everything is and I know for a fact there's never been a drop of laudanum anywhere in this house. So where'd it come from? Did Mrs Grady buy it?'

Cook's face sported a black glare. 'If I thought you're accusing Rosie of suicide—'

'As if I would. What I want to know is how a bottle of laudanum got in her bedroom.'

'Don't look at me, Mary Finch,' Cook said sharply. 'Or at Tobias. And Ella there didn't buy it. Not Fortune, either. And where did that girl go? What was she chasing?'

'If I said spirits, what would you say?'

'You know exactly what I'd say.' Cook huffed and turned back to Mrs Grady.

'Has anyone spoken to anyone other than the coppers about what happened?' Mary asked. 'Did anyone speak to Mr Hawthorne?'

'Do you think anyone would?' Cook said. 'I wouldn't tell that grasping man the time of day—nor would Tobias.'

'Nor would the Inspector,' Mary added.

Cook stared at her. 'What is it?' she asked. 'What do you know that you're not telling me?'

'A lot more now.' Mary grasped the bottle of laudanum. 'Like how this got here. I just don't know why.'

Mrs Grady murmured in her sleep, drenched in sweat, her teeth grinding in her delirium, and Cook turned away to sit beside her friend. Mary thought she heard the old lady ask Cook to let her die. She was tired and wanted to be with Patrick.

Cook gave Mary a firm stare.

'You'll not say a word of that, do you hear me?' she said between gritted teeth. 'It's the delirium. She doesn't know what she's saying.'

Mary turned to Ella. The small girl wore a fierce look and pouted back defiantly.

'All right! I'm sorry!' Mary said understanding the meaning of her angry, sullen eyes. 'I didn't mean to hurt you. I was worried about Fortune. I still am. I'm worried sick, especially as I can't do anything but wait. And I'm fed up with waiting.' She pulled Ella closer. 'Now you're gonna tell me exactly what you saw.'

Ella confessed that she and Fortune met in the kitchen when everyone was asleep. While Fortune was telling her that a new Mrs Grady would be their mistress, they heard someone enter the house. They were afraid when they saw the Grey Lady. Fortune said her doll would protect them, so they followed her up the stairs to Mrs Grady's bedroom. Then they heard Mrs Grady scream. The last she saw was the spirit rushing down the stairs and Fortune following.

'But how did *you* know someone was here?' Ella asked.

'He might not be much of a mouser,' Mary said, nodding to Oscar sitting on one of the attic treads, washing his face. 'But for a cat, he's one hell of a guard dog.'

20

DIRE NEWS

WHEN THE LAST of the police officers departed, Mary paced the rooms like a caged animal. Lestrade's dark and gloomy demeanour did not make her hopeful and she feared greatly for Fortune. She attempted to dust and tidy to keep herself busy, but gave it up as a lost cause. Her mind refused to be switched off. The cogs turning and the wheels rotating and the gears meshing incessantly. With a scream of utter exasperation, she flung down the duster and dustpan.

Going up to her attic room, she sat on her bed, her mind adrift. As the morning slipped away and eased into the afternoon, she gradually became focused and regained control of her thoughts. By then, it was early evening and the room was in darkness.

She lit the oil lamp and turned the wick high. There

were too many things that concerned her. Gathering them up in her mind, she began to sort through them.

On the bed, she placed the photograph taken in the British Museum of a startled Mrs Grady, Mr Barclay and assistants with the reflection of the Grey Lady in the mirror.

'Right! What we have here, Oz, is proof that the Grey Lady exists.' The cat who'd been asleep near her pillow was now alert, and was seated next to her. Beside the picture, she placed the grey rag she had in her hand that day in the museum, the one she mopped the floor with.

'Now, what this proves is the Grey Lady is real and not a spirit, because I tore it from her dress. Of that I'm sure. And you can't tear things from a spirit—at least, I don't think you can.'

The cat walked imperiously across the bed, sniffed the rag and curled his nose. A shiver ran along from his head to his tail.

'But Fortune chased her in the museum and said she vanished—just like that!' Mary squinted and set her jaws firmly. 'I can't explain that, nor all the strange things I saw that day, Oz. Like everyone, I saw the mummy rise from its coffin, when we all know it didn't. And I guess "foul air" might explain that. Only I was well away from any "foul air" when I saw them other things.'

She added a drawing she made of the face of the Grey Lady. It showed a blank, empty, featureless head except for two hollow eyes, black and gaping. But she recalled a sheen they had, like small glass panes were affixed to each.

'Now, Fortune said she saw the Grey Lady running, but I saw her floating when I chased her. Well, that don't make sense—it has to be one or the other. So, tell me this, Oz, when do ghosts leave footprints?' she murmured. 'Or come through French windows? Or force locks? Or make sounds as they run away? One thing is for sure—what happened was no burglary. There was lots to take downstairs and no reason for a thief to chance going upstairs.'

She placed the other photograph of the opening of the tomb, showing the five members of the expedition—*the day they awoke death,* as Mrs Grady said—along with the articles culled from the various newspapers regarding their unexplained deaths.

'Then there's the Denbies.'

She found the playbill Archie took the day they'd visited them, Madame Zanaib and her daughter, Veda— *the oracle knows all, sees all and tells all*—and added that.

'How come she knows so much? Patrick Grady's sins? Him with Mrs Grady in that Inn. Him and that song which only Mrs Grady knows about? Siobhan Fitzwilliam? And even about the Grey Lady before the tomb was opened? And the thing is, Oz, if they're frauds, why aren't they bleeding Mrs Grady dry like a conman would? It took months before they'd even agree to see the old lady again. And they're just as scared about the ghost as everyone else.'

Next on the bed went Fortune's doll, battered and broken, along with Mary's locket.

'And Lorna knew all about Danny and me. Now, I definitely didn't tell her anything about him. She couldn't have known that I'd be visiting her. So, don't all that make her a proper medium?' Mary took a deep breath and sniffed disparagingly. 'But if the Grey Lady's not a ghost, then what does that make them, since it was they who predicted her?'

She shook her head and arranged all the items in chronological order, and then crouched on the edge of the bed.

'Where did the bottle of laudanum come from, Oz? I'll tell you where. From the Grey Lady. Now that'd only make sense if she's flesh and blood, along with the footprints and likes. I think you'd agree, she can't be both a ghost and not.'

Mary stood with her arms folded.

'Then there's what that lawyer said this morning. He'd just arrived at the house. No one said anything to him, yet he knew Mrs Grady had been attacked by the Grey Lady and she'd taken poison.'

Again, Mary crouched, this time beside the bed.

'Tell me something, Oscar,' Mary asked the cat. 'What's going on? If the Grey Lady's no ghost, then what is she? Everything points to the Denbies being crooks, yet lots says they ain't. That lawyer's a crook, though. So, where does that leave us?'

Mary slumped heavily into her armchair and closed her eyes. Fortune Dubois's face drifted into her mind. The ticking of the grandfather clock in the downstairs hallway drifted into her room…

The next thing she knew was the firm knock on the door that awoke her. She must have fallen asleep. The lamp had burned out and the singed wick left a sour tang in the air. The first light of day was falling through the window. It was morning.

When she opened the door, she was staring into the serious eyes of Inspector Lestrade. A frown cut the policeman's face. Behind him stood Cook and Constable O'Connor. The tip of Cook's nose was red and sore, and she clutched a handkerchief to her mouth.

'I have some bad news,' Lestrade said hesitantly. 'I think you had better sit.' In his nervousness, his voice dropped several tones. He swallowed. 'The body of a small girl was pulled from the Thames last night.'

For a second, Mary did not understand his words. Then she clutched the arms of the chair and sprang up.

'Fortune?'

'I fear it is the missing maid,' Lestrade said and nodded solemnly.

Cook whimpered and brought the handkerchief to her eyes, and Constable O'Connor wrapped his arms around her. Mary mumbled something inaudible, the words catching in her throat.

Lestrade sighed heavily. 'Miss Finch, I am afraid I will need someone who knew the young girl to identify her body.' His eyes held a pleading look; he seemed embarrassed. 'Your cook says she would come, but I think under the circumstances, two people would be better. Mr Venables said he would, but I feel that you might want to instead… knowing how you… well, how… I can arrange it for this evening. I think the sooner, the better.'

Mary's stomach churned. She swayed, but ignored the Inspector's proffered arm.

'But is it her?' she whispered, fighting back the tears.

'Yes, I would say it is.' He nodded. 'A small coloured girl, ten, eleven maybe. Long plaited hair tied with a bow. We found this.' Lestrade showed Mary a pair of muddy shoes. Mary recognised them immediately. 'Constable O'Connor found them at the far entrance to the park.'

O'Connor nodded gravely and said, 'There was a witness to a commotion that took place there. A young girl, matching Fortune's description, was dragged into a carriage that went off in a hurry. Some blood was found at the scene.'

Mary steeled herself. No matter how she felt, she must not cry; she had to be strong for Cook's sake. Yet the scullery maid's smiling face filled her mind—how Fortune complained about going to school; how she played with Ella; Cook always glaring at her, but never meaning it. She was cheeky, but always sincere. She cared for Mrs Grady enough to make her a magic doll to protect her. And now Fortune was dead. Chasing after a ghost, she had been murdered.

How would she tell the Dibble children? Each Sunday, Fortune and Ella went and played with them, or they came to Holland Park. Mary had forgotten that in all the excitement. Dot and Sally would be disappointed that neither visited yesterday. And now, Fortune never would again.

Mary held Cook and drew her near. She could feel her heave and swell with sobs as she held her tightly, not knowing what to say.

But she was angry.

The girl was no more than eleven years old.

Mary's quick eyes glanced along the corridor and down the stairs.

Who would tell Ella?

21

OMNE IGNOTUM PRO MAGNIFICO

MARY ASSUMED that Constable O'Connor came with Lestrade especially. He had nearly arrested her on a misunderstanding with her last employer, not two months ago. But since then, Mary and Fortune had seen him often when they went to visit the Dibbles, and they had become good friends. She did not doubt he volunteered for this onerous assignment.

When Lestrade left, O'Connor remained. He rocked back and forth on his heels, as was his habit when he was nervous. Mary was glad he was there. The house was an alien place, inhabited by the ghost of Fortune Dubois. No matter where she looked, Mary saw the small girl—even when she closed her eyes. She could hear her voice calling: *'Miss Mary.'* Whatever happened to the small girl, Mary hoped she had not suffered.

'I suppose you'll be wanting a cup of tea,' Cook said in a hoarse whisper to O'Connor, a brave face covering her fears. 'I've never known a policeman not to want one.'

'A cup would go down a treat, missus,' he said and gave her a small, friendly smile. 'She needs to be busy,' he whispered to Mary when Cook left.

At that, Mary burst into tears. She fell against the Constable.

'There, there, Mary,' he said, somewhat embarrassed. 'It's a bad thing, I know. But you need to be strong for everyone's sake. You're tough as nails. I know that from how you dealt with Black Bob and his mates.'

But this nail had bent, Mary thought, at the first hammering, and she felt it would never be straightened again. Black Bob was different, he was trying to kill her. This seemed a slower death.

Constable O'Connor held her like the father she'd never known until her tears dried and she'd wiped her nose on her sleeve. After she passed a brush through her hair, she sat and gazed blankly ahead. The policeman stood and waited patiently.

'So, what's this odd collection?' he said to make conversation, looking at the items still arranged neatly on the bed. His question brought Mary back to the present.

She shrugged and could only mumble, 'Nothing, just trying to make sense of a puzzle.'

'These here are them that died from the Egyptian curse.' He lifted up the newspaper articles one after each other. 'That gives me the shudders, I must admit.'

Mary nodded slightly.

'Madame Zanaib!' O Connor said brightly and knowingly, picking up the playbill. 'I saw them at the theatre. Now, that was a brilliant act. The things they knew about me and all I did was show them my pocket watch. They knew I was a copper, that I'd been in the Army, where I came from, that I was married—even what I'd had for dinner.'

He smiled shyly. 'It was the best clairvoyant act I have ever seen,' he continued. 'It was as if Veda—her real name's Lorna, did you know? It was as if she read my mind. I mean, their last act was good, but that one was miles better.'

Oh! They were good, all right, Mary thought, *the way they raised all those ghosts.*

'Is she part of your puzzle?'

Mary stood beside the policeman and saw how hard he was trying to help. But her voice was almost a whisper. 'They came and did a séance for the mistress a couple of times,' she said.

'You know, I always reckoned it was a trick—their clairvoyant act, I mean.' O'Connor scratched his head. 'But then I saw they went private and I knew there was more to it than that. Somebody at the Yard investigated and found that they were the actual thing. That girl is real. I mean, she does see things. She read me like a book that day. My old mum would love her to do a séance, if only to find out where Dad hid his railway shares.' He laughed. 'But her last act…'

Mary was aware that O'Connor was looking at her with a kindly expression, and she felt embarrassed at not responding.

'What was her last act?' she asked politely.

'Now, that was hilarious!' A smile broke O'Connor's face, as if he was seeing it before him at that very moment. 'The Four Musketeers. A quick-change comedy act. I took my Nancy there and we laughed so much, we nearly died of stitches.'

He stopped to suppress a laugh.

'There were four of them—three others and her, Madame Zanaib—except she was Mrs Denbie then. You know the type of act I'm talking about? On and off stage, coming back as someone else, tripping over each other, throwing their voices around. Just when you thought one of them would appear from one of the wings, you'd see her running down the aisle and climbing on to the stage —they just sort of appeared dressed differently until you thought there were a dozen of them in the troupe and not four.'

Suddenly, he burst out laughing.

'You should have seen how high my Nancy jumped

when she thought she heard one of the Musketeers shouting next to her! Well, when she comes down off the ceiling—Mrs Denbie, it was her that did it, she was way over the other side of the aisle, throwing her voice.' He wiped tears of laughter from his eyes. 'Ah! But then they broke up. Such a shame. I'd have liked to see them again. Three went back to America because they were home-sick, and Mrs Denbie stayed and became Madame Zanaib and Veda, with her daughter.'

He placed the playbill back where he'd found it.

Mary turned to the window. She looked out, vaguely listening to the policeman. Even when Cook came back with the tea, his words barely touched her.

There were two problems to be solved, she reckoned. The first and most pressing was to exorcise the spirit haunting her mistress. For that, she needed to go back and see the Denbies. There was something odd about the medium and her mother that Mary could not articulate, just as there was something odd about their prediction— the Grey Lady—that troubled her.

The second problem was what would happen when the legal case came before the courts. That was something she could not do anything about. Mrs Grady was in no condition to fight the lawsuit until she regained her reason. It followed, then, that solving the first problem would return Mrs Grady's strength to tackle the second. She would need to be strong to contest the case—Fogarty Hawthorne was determined.

But there was something odd about the snipe, and that troubled Mary as well.

The Denbies. She nodded and whispered their name. Mary hoped Danny would forgive her, but Mrs Grady needed to come first since that was something she could do now—that and supporting poor Cook in identifying the body of her friend.

'Here, Finch, you ain't heard a word I've said, have you?' O'Connor touched her shoulder and Mary turned back in surprise. He was still smiling.

'I'm sorry,' she said. 'I was miles away.'

'To the moon and back, by the looks of you. You all right?' O'Connor asked, looking at how strangely Mary was surveying the items on her bed. 'You look like you've seen a ghost.'

'I just thought about a couple of things Mr Holmes said.' Mary glanced towards him.

'Oh, him! And what's he got to say for himself?' The mention of the detective's name caused a wry smile to appear on the policeman's lips.

'*Omne ignotum pro magnifico.*'

'*Omne... pro...* what?'

'It's Latin!' Mary said.

'It'd have to be if the great Sherlock Holmes said it.' O'Connor laughed. 'And what does it mean when it's at home?'

Mary smiled at him. 'It means something that didn't

make sense, once it's explained, makes perfect sense. And this is beginning to make sense,'

'Yee-essss!' O'Connor replied, 'and the other thing *he* said?'

Mary grinned broadly. 'Well, he didn't say it exactly, only that I should read up about it. Occam's Razor,' she replied.

'What?' and he ran a finger across his chin.

'Tell me, Constable, since when do ghosts leave foot-prints and mud on the stairs?'

The policeman smiled awkwardly and shook his head.

'Or break in by forcing locks?'

O'Connor took her arm.

'Or administer laudanum?'

'Come on, Mary,' he said, dragging her away from her bedroom, 'let's get some more tea and keep your cook company. She's taken all this hard.'

In the kitchen, as they sat in silence and finished their tea, in her mind's eye, Mary again saw the items placed on her bed as clearly as if they were in front of her. She had a notion of a plan. Some of the things that did not made sense seemed to be finally doing so. Her fingers drummed on the kitchen table. In a roundabout way, things were falling into place—even the death of Fortune Dubois.

'*Sergeant* O'Connor,' she smiled a Cheshire Cat grin —since he had arrested her at the Grimwigs', and the promotional prospects he'd thought that would bring did not materialised, his rank had become a private joke between them.

O'Connor slowly closed his eyes, took a deep breath and shook his head knowingly. 'Yes! Miss Finch?'

'Can I cadge a lift to Baker Street?'

22

A STRANGE MEETING

TO HER ANNOYANCE, when Mary arrived in Baker Street, Mrs Hudson informed her that Mr Holmes and Dr Watson were away on a case and unlikely to be back for several days. She spent a few minutes nursing her disappointment while seated on the front step.

It was all so clear in her mind when she left the house in Holland Park. See Mr Holmes. Tell him the facts. Say what she thought they meant. Listen to his reasoning. Then act accordingly. Now—not for the first time in her life—she had to rely on her own resources.

She went down the street to see the Dibbles and was glad that Dot and Sally were still at school and only Grandma, Grandpa and Archie were there. She took Archie aside and told him the sad news, and as she did so, the dreadful thought played in her mind that Fortune was murdered because she found something out about the Grey Lady when she chased her into Holland Park. Mary shivered at the idea of having to identify the poor scullery maid's body.

She forced such thoughts from her mind and told Archie her plans—to visit the solicitor, Mr Hawthorne, and then go and see the Denbies. When she finished speaking, her mouth firmed, and her brows furrowed as she gazed intently at the floor. Then, when her fingers drummed the table, Archie moaned.

'This is trouble, ain't it?' he said. 'I've seen that look before. The last time it nearly got you killed.'

'I can't explain it all, at least not fully,' she said, 'but something is dreadfully wrong, Archie. Ghosts don't leave footprints. They don't open doors. They don't wear dresses that tear. They don't run away or bash you. And they don't leave bottles of laudanum about and make people drink the stuff.'

'Laudanum? What're you going on about?' When Mary told him, Archie whispered, 'Mrs Grady nearly did herself in?'

'Don't you believe it!' Mary stood indignantly in front of him. 'She's poorly. She's a wreck. Her health has gone downhill since the start of all this. But don't you believe that for one second.' She tugged Archie's sleeve. 'It was when that snipe came and knew all the things that happened that night, without being told them—that's what got me thinking.'

'And you aim to find out how he knew?' he said, already knowing the answer.

Archie found his coat and they walked towards Soho in silence. Mr Hawthorne's office was somewhere on Greek Street. Surely it would be an easy enough task to find which house by reading the brass plaques on or beside each of the doors? However, almost as soon as they turned into the street, the unmistakable figure of Fogarty Hawthorne, dressed in black, exited a door several houses ahead of them. He stood waiting in the street. Mary started towards him, then stopped. Another man joined the solicitor. In a deft motion, and much to Archie's surprise, she spun him around and pushed him under the awning of a shop doorway.

'What're you doing?' Archie asked.

Mary flicked her chin towards the solicitor. 'Look! Those two men…' she said.

'But, ain't that Mrs Denbie's fa—? But I—' Archie stuttered. Mary pulled him around, to make it appear as if they were looking at something in the shop window. 'But I thought…'

Mary hushed him and pressed further under the awning. She peered over his shoulder: next to the solic- itor stood Mrs Denbie's father. Both men glanced in their direction and started walking towards them. For a moment, she thought about entering the shop when she heard the old man laugh. Her heart thumped, fearing they had been seen. She watched the reflection of the two men in the windowpane and saw the solicitor pass over a cigarette. A match flared. The old man leant forward to catch the flame and straightened up to blow a stream of smoke into the air. He said something and it was Hawthorne's turn to laugh.

They came nearer, and Mary shuffled closer to Archie. To her horror, the two men stopped just beside them. The old man drew deeply on the cigarette and exhaled again. Then they walked on, deep in conversation. Soon they reached a corner and turned. Immediately, Mary started to follow them.

'But I thought—I mean—' Archie scratched his head in confusion.

'That he was dying?' Mary remembered the frail, coughing person they met a few days earlier, spitting blood into a handkerchief; his hand trembling as if he had palsy; his weak croaking voice.

'Yes! Consumption!' Archie nodded.

'Well, he's made a speedy recovery, ain't he?' Mary snapped. 'And that's the lawyer with him who threatened Mrs Grady.'

'So they know each other?' Archie asked.

Mrs Denbie's father and Mr Hawthorne were ambling along slowly. There was something friendly in the way they walked, their gestures, their easy demeanour in each other's company that Mary could not help but notice. Grasping Archie's hand, she furrowed her brow and firmed her chin determinedly.

'I can't explain it,' she whispered. 'Look, Archie, I don't know how Lorna Denbie knows all that stuff about Mrs Grady, ghosts and me. But everything comes back to them. It was them that predicted the Grey Lady. It was them that predicted that Patrick Grady's first wife would come back. It was them that knew all about Patrick and Mrs Grady when they got married.'

'Which is why she's a medium and you ain't,' Archie said.

'But it only makes sense if the Grey Lady is a ghost, don't you see? She ain't! She's as real as you and me. There's a trick here. It was something O'Connor said about Lorna Denbie reading him like a book. It's the sort of thing Mr Holmes does.'

'But what you're on about only makes sense if they're conning Mrs Grady—which they clearly ain't.'

He was right, of course. Mary shook her head. That didn't make sense. However, seeing the old man with the solicitor fuelled her growing distrust for the Denbies.

'Do you remember seeing some photographs in the old man's room when we visited the Denbies?''

Archie shook his head. 'All I remember is seeing him coughing his lungs out and feeling sorry for him,' he said ruefully. 'What pictures?'

'There was one of him when he was a sailor. I didn't think much of it at the time. For the life of me, I can't recall it properly. Seeing the old man dying like that, and

what happened with Lorna and my locket, took my attention away. I want to see them again.'

It soon became clear that the two men were cutting
through Soho towards Berwick Street. When they arrived
at the Denbies' flat, Mary and Archie slipped back into
the shadow of a doorway and waited. Though she was
determined to see the photographs again, she would not
do it as long as Mr Hawthorne was there. She would wait
for him to leave.

'Once we're in, I'll tell them Mrs Grady wants
another séance,' Mary said, 'which won't be far from the
truth, and we'll take it from there. I'll contrive to see the
pictures somehow.'

She knew that when they knocked, the surly maid
would answer and keep them waiting, just long enough
for the Denbies to prepare their little charade. The old
man in bed and dying of consumption, no doubt, as his
daughter and granddaughter acted their part in the drama.

Ten minutes passed, and then the door opened. The
old man and Mr Hawthorne came out and stood idly by.
Soon, Mrs Denbie and her daughter joined them. Not
long afterwards, the maid came out. The party crossed
the street and moved away.

Mary recalled that each Monday afternoon, the
Denbies held consultations in private rooms somewhere
in Soho. For a moment, she was at a loss as to what to do.
Strolling across the street to the Denbie's flat, she
glanced in both directions. Much to Archie's surprise, she

gave the door a hefty shove. It was solid and barely moved.

'What are you doing?' Archie asked, glancing about him nervously.

No one paid them any attention, so Mary grabbed his arm and hurried him along to a side alley by the building. A high brick wall separated the alley from the house. The mortar on the top of the wall was embedded with broken glass to deter burglars. Mary reached up carefully in an attempt to climb the wall.

Archie grabbed her.

'What's the game?' he whispered.

'I'm going in,' Mary said. 'Come on, give me a leg up.'

'Breaking in? You mad?'

Mary gave him a stare that said she was serious.

23

THE BREAK-IN THAT WAS

ARCHIE LIFTED his eyes to the sky and shook his head in resignation, then looked to either side to see if anyone was watching. He looked back to Mary. She looked grimly resolved. Removing his coat, he folded it and slung it across the sharp glass, and then cupped his hands together for her to step into.

She climbed up carefully, stepping on to his coat. When he joined her, they climbed across to a sloping bay roof adjacent to the wall, just below a window. Mary tried the window, but it was closed.

When she took off her shawl and wrapped it around her fist, Archie moaned.

'Bleedin' hell, Mary,' he said and took a deep breath, 'we can get arrested for this.'

'Don't you think it's curious that Mrs Denbie's supposedly dying father knows Hawthorne?' Mary whispered. 'I thought there was something wrong before, but seeing them with the lawyer, I *know* there's something wrong. Now, come on, give me a hand before they come back, because I'm going in!'

She raised her fist to smash the glass. Archie grabbed her arm.

'If we have to break in, let's do it properly, at least,' he said and took out a penknife. He slipped the blade between the two halves of the sash window and dragged it hard against the swinging latch. It took a minute; the blade scraped and scratched and bit deeply, slowly moving the latch aside. Pushing the window up and climbing through, he reached out an arm and Mary grasped it.

Even though she knew the house was empty, Mary's heart thumped wildly. Her legs trembled, and as Archie pulled her up, she was sweating with excitement and terror.

'I hope you know what *we're* doing,' Archie said, glancing out of the window and down to the alley. No one had seen them.

They were standing in what appeared to be Mrs Denbie's bedroom. It was a plain room with plain furniture and a small bed, and the wardrobe door was open. On the bed was a grey dress. Mary noticed a tear at the hem that had been repaired. She gave Archie a wide smile and lifted up the hem to show him. He shrugged and Mary rolled her eyes.

'But ain't this dress strange?' he said, holding it up. It was cloak-like. The wearer would not step into it, but would wrap it around herself instead. Yet once it was on it would look, to all intents and purposes like a complete dress. The buttons and stays were no more than decorations; they had no function and could not be opened or closed. However, with the dress wrapped around the wearer, they would appear to complete the garment. The inside of the dress was black with the same decorations, so it could be worn either way out. In the wardrobe were similar garments.

'Don't you see?' Mary said. 'This is how she does it, how she vanishes.'

Mary ignored the puzzled look on Archie's face and wrapped the dress around herself. It was far too long and draped on the floor, but it seemed to be a real dress. In an instant, she slipped it off, reversed it and was now wearing black.

'Get it?' she asked and he nodded enthusiastically.

Putting the dress back as they'd found it, they slipped through into the sitting room. On this occasion, the curtains were fully open. The room looked pleasant enough and the posters could be seen in detail.

'That was Mrs Denbie before she became Madame Zanaib.' Mary pointed to a poster of the Four Fabulous Musketeers. 'O'Connor told me they were a quick-change comedy act.'

Archie flicked his eyes back to Mrs Denbie's room.

'Yes, exactly!' Mary nodded.

'Let's find those pictures and get out of here,' Archie whispered nervously.

Mary opened the door to old man's room and cautiously peeped in. She kept on casting anxious looks over her shoulders as if expecting him to appear suddenly.

The room was dark. The bed was made up. Any hints that it once contained a very ill man were missing. Her nervousness compelled her to glance behind the curtains and through the open window to the street below in case the Denbies were returning. Berwick Street was its usual self, busy with traders and shoppers, the humming of their voices rising up into the room.

She knelt down beside the small cabinet under the window. It looked like a shrine of some sort when she'd first seen it, complete with photographs, candles and religious objects. But it was changed. The photographs were stacked on top of each other or leaning against the wall. The small porcelain statue of Christ and the standing crucifix were pushed away, along with the candle. Everything was packed up.

The first two photographs she looked at had been taken recently. They were of the grandfather, mother and Lorna, along with the maid. Oddly, the maid was as finely dressed as the other three. She posed just as easily as they did, and curiously, her arm was around Lorna's waist.

Then came a photograph of several men on a quay-side. It was a much older picture than the first two. Mary thought one of the men could have been Mrs Denbie's father when he was younger. The next photograph was another of the several men. Again, they were on a quay-side. Mary's heart fluttered and beat uneasily when she saw what was behind the men.

'What is it?' Archie peered over.

Mary raised the print to see it in a better light. The photograph must have been over thirty years old. Even though it was fuzzy and grey, one of the men was Mrs Denbie's father. Of that she was sure, now she could see the image more clearly. He bore the unmistakable features of the person she had seen ailing in the bed not so long ago. The others in the image she did not recognise, with the exception of someone who looked uncannily like Mr Venables. He was finely clothed, unlike the others; his hair was so blond as to be almost white. She held it closer still. He was not a sailor and stood slightly apart from them as they posed under the prow of a ship.

'It's Patrick Grady's ship. It's the *Jane Rose*. Look!' Mary said excitedly.

At the edge of the photograph, and half concealed, was the ship's name. The word 'ROSE' could just be made out. Her fingers tingled in anticipation as she carefully placed the photographs back. She clenched her fist in triumph—the dress, and now the photograph.

'What's this?' Archie said and he startled. His face

went pale. He was holding a small, battered doll made from coarse hessian that he had removed from the cabinet. An upside-down red heart was sewn on the front; an arm of the doll was a dark red stain.

Mary snatched it from him. Wisps of wiry black hair were glued to the sides of the head.

'It's one of Fortune's dolls,' she whispered. Fortune must have made three: one for Mary, another for Mrs Grady, and a third for herself. 'She was here, Archie.'

She looked up at the boy. They both had the same thought. Her mouth gaped in horror.

'That's blood, ain't it?' He touched the stain.

Mary's stomach twisted sharply. She fought back a wave of nausea and stuffed the doll into her pocket angrily. There was a grim look on her face as she delved deeper inside the cupboard where Archie found it.

Mary pulled out a set of scales, together with some weights and several small bottles. One said 'Hemlock', which she knew was a poison. Another, 'Mandrake Roots'. That was a poison, too. A third was faded and stained, and she thought it read 'Ginseng', something she did not know. Some more bottles with equally faded labels were next to it. One bottle was unlabelled and contained some powder that smelled faintly of violets.

She held it in her hand and screwed up her brow in thought. This was the fourth time she remembered that smell. Once when the Denbies did the séance. Once at the

British Museum when she confronted the Grey Lady. There was a hint of it after Mrs Grady's *accident* with the laudanum. But the first time was in Professor Cavendish's hospital room, that sweet smell mingling with the Carbolic.

'You all right?' Archie asked.

Mary stared into space. Her mind wandered between the photograph, the bottle and the grey dress in Mrs Denbie's bedroom. What had Constable O'Connor said about the Four Musketeers? She picked up the photograph of the men beside the quayside, next to the *Jane Rose*, and scrutinised it, looking at all the faces in turn. Her breath caught in her throat just as a voice rang out from behind her.

'Give me that!'

Mary and Archie swung around. The Denbie's maid dashed towards them. Before Archie could react, she pushed him away and grabbed Mary's hands. Mary was thrown back hard against the open window. She held the photograph up and away, but to her surprise, the maid was tugging and pulling at her other hand, prising the bottle from it.

'Let go, you—' the maid swore. She snarled nastily as she dug in her nails, drawing blood.

Mary yelled in pain. Her grip opened and the bottle fell. The maid grabbed at it and missed. They both watched as it bounced off the edge of the window frame toppling into the street below. The maid leant out of the window, her hands flailing, still trying to grasp it, but the bottle crashed and shattered on the pavement.

The maid swore a hideous curse, and then froze. She looked terrified. Seizing her chance, Mary slipped out from under her and rushed towards the door. Archie, scrambling to his feet, followed. He propelled her through the door and into the sitting room. The maid turned and gave chase.

As they charged back towards Mrs Denbie's bedroom, a clatter of footsteps came from the stairs. The old man, Mrs Denbie's father, waving a cane, was rushing up towards them. Mary pushed Archie into the room and slammed the door shut. She grabbed a chair and jammed it under the doorknob. An instant later, the maid was hammering her fists against the door, twisting the knob and shouting abuse at them.

Gritting her teeth and fighting back her fears, Mary climbed through the window and quickly stepped from the sloping roof onto the wall. Jumping down, she sprawled across the pavement. Archie followed. In his hurry, he slipped and howled in pain. He'd gashed his knee and when he landed with a heavy thump, he wailed again, clutching his ankle. Mary dragged him upright and he limped heavily as they went back into Berwick Street.

To their utter surprise, the street was in uproar. People were running and screaming and shouting as if mad. They were fighting with each other, pushing and shoving, exchanging punches. Some huddled and cringed against the walls as if hiding themselves as well as they could. They pulled their hair, wailed loudly and broke out into tears. Others on the opposite side of the street stood perplexed and watched the sudden mayhem that infected their neighbours, before joining in themselves. The last time Mary saw such madness was in the British Museum.

'Stop, thief!' someone was shouting.

Mary looked up. Mrs Denbie's father, leaning out of his window, was pointing at them. At that moment, the front door flew open and Fogarty Hawthorne rushed out into the street.

'Stop them!' the old man shouted to the solicitor.

Hawthorne made to advance, and then stopped. He began backing away, slowly and carefully; his hand came up to his mouth and nose. He ignored Mary and Archie, despite the old man's plea from the window to 'Get them'. Instead, Hawthorne turned and ran. The street behind him was in pandemonium.

24

THE CHASE

It was no use; they could go no further into Berwick Street, not with such a commotion taking place. Fearful that the old man or the maid would soon appear, Mary and Archie dodged down the alley by the side of the house, Archie wincing in pain with each step. From behind them came what she'd feared—the clatter of shoes on stone that said they were being chased. Desperately, they pushed on, down another alley, across a road and into a further dark passageway. Whoever was behind them was gaining. She urged Archie to hurry.

She wanted to head towards Oxford Street, figuring that in that busy avenue, they would be safe. Instead, she was taking Archie deeper into Soho, where the houses rose up to lean over them and the streets were tapered, dark and empty of people. Above them, the sky was no more than a bright, narrow strip between the roofs.

Archie was slowing, grimacing each time he placed any weight on his hurt ankle. She held him tightly as they fled from one dark alley only to burst into another one. To her dismay, she was lost.

Archie stopped. He pulled a face and slid down onto the ground. His ankle was swollen and the blood from his cut knee ran down his leg.

'Come on,' Mary shouted desperately. She grasped under his armpits and heaved, but the boy was heavy and she barely moved him. She glanced back anxiously. The padding footsteps were coming nearer.

'I can't!' Archie screwed up his face. 'I think I've sprained it.'

'We can't stay.'

Suddenly, she became aware of another uproar. A police whistle was blowing. She heard another, and then yet another. Several policemen rushed past, ignoring her and Archie. She could hear loud cries, as if a riot was taking place, and realised that they had gone in a circle and were almost back where they'd started, in Berwick Street.

'Try, Archie, come on, try,' Mary said, having gained her bearings. Once more, she grasped Archie under his armpits and heaved. With an effort, he struggled up.

As he became upright, the old man appeared. He was panting heavily, his face red from the chase. His eyes fell on to the blood soaking Archie's knee and a nasty smile curled his lips. The old man lifted up his cane and pulled on it. It came away with a click, sliding back to reveal the long, thin blade of a sword.

He hesitated as several policemen dashed past the mouth of the alley. His doubts lasting no more than a second, he rushed towards Mary and Archie.

With one supreme effort, Mary heaved and pushed and dragged Archie into Berwick Street. An instant later, they sprawled across the pavement in front of Constable O'Connor. Through the corner of her eye, she saw the old man freeze and retreat quickly into the deep shadows behind him.

The burly policeman had hold of a small, wild-eyed woman. She was beating her fists against him; as if a gnat was trying to swat an elephant, she barely troubled him. When he noticed Archie's bloody knee, he dropped the woman into the hands of another Constable and came over to them.

'What happened to him?' O'Connor asked Mary.

'Get him!' Mary shouted. She pointed to the alley. 'Get that old man, he's got a sword. He's trying to kill us. He killed Fortune—get him—'

'All right, I will. After I take care of this,' O'Connor said. Amid the utter confusion on the street, he quietly and efficiently began wrapping a large handkerchief around Archie's cut knee. Mary grabbed his shoulder. She shook him, troubling him no more than the wild-eyed woman had. Shouting at him, asking what he was doing, but he was unmoving and steadfast in his task. Without rushing, O'Connor tied the ends of the handkerchief into a knot.

'There, that'll hold until it can get done proper,' he said. 'Might need stitches. Now, what seems to be the problem?' He turned to Mary.

'The old man who lives here, he tried to kill us—Mrs Denbie's father,' Mary shouted frantically.

'Of course, he did,' O'Connor said, his voice almost fatherly.

'He killed Fortune.'

'Did he, indeed? Mrs Denbie's father, you say?'

'They must have killed all those other people.'

'Uh-huh! Of course, they must have.'

'Listen to me!' Mary tugged at his arm angrily, trying to drag him to where the old man had been. 'See?' She pulled out Fortune's doll. 'They had this.'

'Mary.' Archie took her arm and shook her. 'Look!' and he nodded to the street. The uproar and the clamour continued around them. Several Constables were struggling with a number of people. A woman was screaming about seeing snakes. 'Get them off me!' she pleaded, continually brushing her hands over her hair. A man was swinging his fists at nothing, a wild, terrified look in his eyes. People were running about, trying to hide, to escape, each seeing some horror just in front of them. A madness infected the crowd. Even some of the policemen seemed disturbed.

'He thinks we're barmy like them,' Archie explained.

Mary glanced up and saw the kind, smiling eyes of O'Connor looking at her. She stared at the utter chaos. Archie was right: the policeman must have thought her mad. When she looked back, the old man was no longer there. Hawthorne had gone as well.

'Oh, *Sergeant* O'Connor,' Mary moaned and slumped in frustration, tugging at his arm again. 'I need to see Inspector Lestrade. Take us to him!'

'He's a busy man,' O'Connor said.

'Humour her,' Archie said. 'Trust me, she won't take no for an answer.'

O'Connor screwed up his eyes as he stared at her. Then he nodded.

'All right, Finch, I knows you well enough, I suppose,' he said and flicked his head to the ruckus happening behind him. 'But only after I finish dealing with this.'

As he turned back, Mary slowly got up. She took a deep breath and held the crook of her arm across her nose and mouth. Walking rapidly along the street, through the centre of the commotion, she stopped under the old man's bedroom window on the first floor. She knelt down, brushed something into her handkerchief and came back, her face turning red. As she exhaled and took a deep breath, there was a scent of violets in the air.

MY BREATH IS DEATH

LESTRADE SAT IN CONTEMPLATIVE SILENCE. He rested his chin on the back of his hand, his elbow on his desk, carefully scrutinising Mary as she spoke. Opposite them, a police surgeon was busy bandaging Archie's sprained ankle, having tended the cut to his knee.

'Look, I know it's hard to believe, but it's true,' she said, exasperated. Mary, who had spent a good half hour explaining what happened and what she knew worried that the delay only gave the Denbies time to get away. 'They are conning people. All that stuff about curses and avenging angels of death, they made it up. Mrs Denbie *is* the Grey Lady. They set this all up. It was them that killed those men from the expedition. They must have murdered Fortune as well because she found out. Mrs Denbie's father would have murdered us if it hadn't been for Constable O'Connor.'

'Let's assume that what you say is true,' Lestrade said quietly. 'What's their motive? Money? Well, it can't be that, can it? You told me how they resolutely refused payment from Mrs Grady. Why didn't they say, "Pay me a hundred pounds, and we'll lift the curse"? And abra-cadabra, whoosh, it's gone and they're a hundred pounds the better off."

'I don't know,' Mary moaned.

'I'm willing to grant that there's a trick here some-where—the dress you describe, for instance, black one side, grey the other. I can see how it could be used in a quick-change act to confuse. Perhaps—and, of course, you may have considered this possibility already—but perhaps she used it in her act when she was one of the Four Musketeers,' he said with not a slight degree of sarcasm. 'But murder? For what gain? I ask once more.' Lestrade gazed at the ceiling as if a little bored. 'As for the mass hallucination the journalists had at the British Museum, Mr Barclay explained that: bad air. And your vision and the boy's? Well, by your own admission, you have been thinking about your brother, and your friend about his mother. Is it any wonder you saw them?' Before Mary could reply, Lestrade held up a hand to quiet her.

'And the same could be said for Mrs Grady. She saw what she wanted to see during the séance. That is how these tricks work: a suggestion here, a suggestion there. Really, Miss Finch, we've been here before. You should leave detection to the professionals instead of wandering down some flight of fancy and making unwarranted accusations of murder.'

'But don't you see, Inspector—'

'And who is to say Lorna Denbie doesn't have some ability? As you yourself have said, how could she have known about something happening three thousand miles away, and then conjure up a grey lady the next day?'

Mary shrugged. She was hot and annoyed and frustrated about not being taken seriously.

'What about Mr Hawthorne?' she said. 'He was with the Denbies, and he knew Patrick Grady's first wife was still alive—'

'And could have told them! Yes, a conspiracy wouldn't surprise me,' Lestrade said smugly.

'Look, Inspector, just yesterday at Mrs Grady's house, you must have heard Mr Hawthorne mention a ghostly grey lady attacking the mistress and that Mrs Grady poisoned herself. How did he know all of that? I didn't tell him. You didn't, nor did Mr Venables nor Cook. He'd only just turned up to the house, so no one could have told him.'

'What are you suggesting?' Lestrade was clearly getting irritated.

'But don't you see?'

'Even though Hawthorne is as dodgy a solicitor as ever there was, he would not stoop to murder. If there's a goal here, then I fail to see it.' Lestrade shook his head. 'What other proof do you have that they are working together? None, I suspect, other than seeing them walking side by side.'

Mary racked her brain. Mrs Denbie's father and the lawyer were connected, she was certain. But Lestrade was sitting in front of her with a superior smirk on his face that annoyed her intensely.

'So what is the point?' he said and sat back in his chair, folding his arms. 'There's no motive. Why kill all those people? *If they did.* Just to give Lorna Denbie's act credence? Come, come. And kill Fortune because she may have found out who the Grey Lady was? To hide a trick? No, no, Miss Finch, this will not do. You've been hanging around Mr Holmes and Dr Watson for too long. They also have fanciful notions.'

Mary slumped back and gazed at the floor. Lestrade was speaking to her as if she was a child and that annoyed her even further.

'The deaths of the expedition members were unfortunate accidents.' He shook his head firmly and decisively. 'No one was poisoned, no one was stabbed or shot or pushed or strangled or... or... That's why we have coroners,' he said bluntly. 'It was a coincidence that a woman dressed in grey was present on each occasion. Just go to the window, Miss Finch. How many women wearing grey or whitish dresses are walking down the street at this very moment?'

'At least go to Berwick Street and see for yourself,' Mary pleaded.

'And there's another case of bad air,' Lestrade said dismissively. 'Men were working in the sewers there only this morning.'

'And ain't it convenient that it happens around the Denbies?' Mary barked.

Lestrade stood and leant across the desk on his arms.

'Convenience is not evidence or confirmation of a crime,' he said slowly as if trying to maintain some control. 'There is no proof that Mrs Denbie, or her father, murdered Fortune, or anyone else for that matter.' He waved his hand as if to dismiss Mary. 'Now I have a *real* crime to deal with.'

'And the doll?' Mary asked curtly.

The policeman gave a deep sigh of irritation.

'Something Mrs Denbie may have picked up when she was last at Mrs Grady's? Something to add to her act in the future? I have no doubt there's an innocent explanation,' and he dropped his head and began reading from the file on the desk.

'But Inspector, Fortune only made those dolls after the séance.'

'I am busy, young lady,' Lestrade interrupted smoothly. 'Why not tell your tale to Mr Holmes, and he can investigate this fancy? *I* am busy investigating Fortune Dubois's murder.' He waved his open palm to the door, inviting her to leave, and glared at Constable O'Connor.

Mary slumped heavily into a chair outside Lestrade's

office, staring at the floor. Her face burned in anger. O'Connor came back with a cup of tea for her and tried to soothe her ruffled feathers.

'Look, Mary, you've been under stress, and stress does strange things. I mean, when I was fighting with my regiment in Afghanistan, it was so hot and I was so thirsty, I thought I saw all sorts of devils. And you're understandably worried about going to the morgue and seeing the maid's body.'

'I've never been to Afghanistan, it ain't hot and I'm not thirsty,' Mary grunted. 'And I'm not seeing devils, nor am I stressed about seeing Fortune's body.'

She glanced nervously at Archie. She might be able to fool O'Connor, but not her friend—she *was* worried.

'I didn't imagine seeing that old man ill in bed—nor did Archie. Nor him coming at me with a sword. Nor the other things. And I bloomin' well will go and see Mr Holmes and he'll believe me,' she growled. 'I helped him out once, did you know that? He trusts me and respects me. He knows that I don't imagine things. He'll know that I didn't just see things because I was *stressed.*' She glared at Archie, who was laughing. 'And I thought you was my friend,' she huffed.

'Don't shoot me as well. I told Lestrade about the old man coming at us with a sword, didn't I? You're lucky he didn't do us for breaking and entering.'

'Ah! There's that, Mary,' O'Connor said. 'He'll have

to if and when the Denbies complain. And they will, I suspect. Unfortunately, that'll be no illusion.'

Mary folded her arms tightly and gazed down at her lap, grinding her teeth.

'Seeing things, am I?' she said under her breath. 'Visions? Illusions? Devils, is that it? Oh, you're so gonna hate me, Lestrade.' She got to her feet quickly. 'Really hate me, and I don't need to be a mind reader to predict that.'

'Oh, dear me,' Archie groaned. 'I've seen that look before, and believe me when I say it ain't good.'

Mary reached inside her pocket and took out her handkerchief, turned on her heels sharply and walked back into Lestrade's office without knocking. She placed a hand on the table, leaning over towards him. His angry face came up to meet hers.

He scowled, barking, 'Miss Finch—!'

'My breath is death,' Mary whispered to him. She lifted up the handkerchief and blew the dust she had picked up from under the Denbies' window into his face. Immediately, the air was scented with violets. Mary quickly stepped back to the door, holding her breath.

'I swear, if you do not get out of my office—' Lestrade stopped. 'I swear if you... this... this... very... min...' His eyes widened. 'I...'

Then he tensed and screamed.

26

THE MAGIC DUST

LESTRADE'S EYES blazed with fury. Almost immediately, his face was slick with sweat. He rose quickly, knocking over his chair, and edged back to the far wall of his office. His eyes flicked right and left, and he balled his fists and raised his arms. Without another pause, he thrashed out wildly as if fighting some invisible foe that came at him from the corner.

'Get him off of me!' he screamed. 'Stop him before he kills me! Help! Help! Help!'

Hearing his shouts, O'Connor, followed by two others, burst into the room, only to stand rooted to the spot. Lestrade flew at them. O'Connor easily spun him around and tackled him to the ground and, with the two sturdy Constables restrained the Inspector's arms and legs, thus keeping him from harm. All the time, Lestrade shouted orders for them to protect him from some terrible beast. The Constables looked perplexed, but held on to him grimly.

Mary watched open-mouthed and thoroughly fascinated, but concerned, too. She saw such dynamism once before: Lestrade was behaving exactly the way Professor Cavendish had in Charing Cross Hospital. She became worried, remembering how the professor tried to hurl himself from the window. The three policemen, however, pinned Lestrade to the floor. While the other two held his thrashing legs, O'Connor threw himself across the Inspector's chest.

'What have you done?' Archie said. 'Are you mad? He'll have you arrested.'

The corridor outside the office quickly filled with people anxious to see what was going on. O'Connor shouted for Mary to close the door. He and the other Constables wrestle with the Inspector for a good five minutes, before his madness wore off in fits and starts, and he began to calm. After a while, he stopped struggling altogether, but every now and then a shadow would darken the Inspector's eyes and he'd growl and strain again. The Constables, fearing some trick, did not release him. Only when he barked their names several times and ordered them to *'Get off me, you idiots!'* did they let go. And even then, they did so carefully, ready to leap on him again should he be tricking them.

Rather than getting up, Lestrade eased back against the wall by the window and seated on the floor stared menacingly towards Mary. He clutched his head as if it was bursting and licked his parched lips with a dry tongue; he was drenched in sweat.

'I'm sorry, Inspector,' Mary said softly.

She approached him tentatively; a little afraid of the acidic glare he was giving her, and took his hand. She completely understood how he felt. It was not unlike how she'd felt that day at the museum.

'But don't you see? The Denbies are tricking people. That dust I blew into your face was how they made us see what we all saw at the museum, and the séance. It's some sort of… I don't know… magic powder—'

'Hallucinogenic,' Lestrade said sourly. 'Some opiate that…' He shook his head as if to clear the smoke and dust from his brain and his eyes flicked like he was seeing something in the corner of his room.

'She did the same to me—the Grey Lady,' Mary said. 'I only realised that was what happened when I saw the dress with a tear and those other things in the flat. And when I saw how the people were behaving in the street where the bottle smashed, then I knew for certain. And each time I was with the Grey Lady, I smelt that smell.'

Lestrade mumbled, 'Violets!'

Mary helped him as he shuffled up and sat uneasily on his chair and gripped the table as if he, or it, might collapse at any moment.

'Please, sir, I know what I did was wrong,' Mary said quietly, unable to look the Inspector in the eye, 'and I've no excuses, but—'

Lestrade raised his hand for silence.

'I am by nature a practical man, Miss Finch,' he said calmly, groaning a dry retch, 'and as such, I require evidence to bring before the law. I would be the laughingstock of Scotland Yard were I to relate my visions to a magistrate. And all of your *magic powder* seems to have gone, so we cannot examine it. But I do take your point, though I would have wished you'd found another way of making it.'

'Can't you go to Berwick Street and arrest them and question them? I don't know what their game is, but I know they had something to do with Fortune's murder.'

Mary knew Sherlock Holmes regarded Lestrade as an energetic person. She now saw his determination. Perhaps it was what he had seen while under the influence of the powder, or perhaps a desire to explain it, but he ordered a four-wheeler and sent a message to Bow Street police station to have men meet him in Berwick Street.

On the way, Mary once again explained as much as she knew, as well as she could. Lestrade taking deep breaths, gazed steadily at her.

'The first rule of crime detection, Miss Finch, is to discover the motive. It is usually money, but in this instance, money it is not.' He chewed the inside of his cheeks in contemplation. 'Such an elaborate deception, though, must mean something—I grant you that at least,' and he gave her a grumpy smile.

27

THE PREY HAS FLOWN

To Mary's disappointment, and confirming her fears, the Berwick Street flat was deserted. The Denbies had left hastily. The shopkeepers from across the road confirmed the hurry of their departure. Things they did not have time to pack lay strewn about the rooms. Drawers had been pulled out and emptied. Cupboard doors were left open, shelves bare. They appeared to have taken just the things they could carry, and the dresses were gone, the photographs, the poisons, were all gone.

As Mary wandered about the silent flat, her heart sank. They were practised, Mary understood that; theatre people, always moving from one engagement to another, needed to be organised. Each room was in the same state —efficiently cleared. Even the maid's room. Of course, she had to be involved with the deception; how could she not be? The maid knew the importance of the bottle containing the magic dust, that was why she'd wanted it so badly.

That they were frauds sat heavily. Even so, Mary wondered how Lorna knew so much, not just about Mrs Grady, but also about her. She conceded that Patrick Grady's life, the awful thing he had done, was knowledge that could be obtained with some research. And of course, they would know of Siobhan Fitzwilliam through Mr Hawthorne—such knowledge gave credence to Lorna's vision. Yet, how did Lorna know about the words Patrick sung and said to Mrs Grady? Things that the old lady never spoke of to anyone, let alone about her brother, Danny?

So many things made sense, and so many did not.

However, if the Denbies were gone, at least that part of Mrs Grady's problems was solved. There would be no more Grey Lady, no more séances and deceptions, no more deaths. Such a frightful cost had been levied in giving credibility to this deception, but the hurried way the flat had been vacated suggested the Denbies knew the game was up. Lestrade said he would send out their descriptions, but Mary was certain, with makeup and disguises, things they were familiar with, they would blend into the crowd and vanish.

Mrs Grady could now get her strength back and leave her husband to rest undisturbed, as much as his past would allow. But other problems would occupy her: the spectre of Siobhan Fitzwilliam and the threat of penury. Fogarty Hawthorne would still press his case. A crook he might be, but knowing the Denbies was not illegal.

Mary gazed silently out of the window; her heart sank deep as she struggled to breathe. Berwick Street had returned to normal. No commotion; no people howling and cowering. The wind blew the dust away from the pavement. Even so, there was still a hint of violets in the air.

And then there was Fortune.

Mary shivered. Her limbs felt heavy with the memory. A dreadful task awaited her that she would happily let pass if she could. But for Cook's sake, she must be strong. The nail must be straightened once more. She hoped Archie would accompany her to the Charing Cross morgue. But his sprained ankle and slashed knee suggested he should be at home and she could not ask him when he was in such pain.

Home, she realised, was suddenly an unknown. Would it still be the Rose Garden? Before long, Hawthorne would arrive with his lawsuit and strip Mrs Grady of everything. She would lose her position in society; she would be reduced to poverty; she would become an object of ridicule. A stranger would occupy the house. But without Fortune there, it would be a strange place, anyway.

'Miss Mary, Miss Mary,' Fortune's voice flooded her mind. She smiled at the exotic accent; she always wanted to ask Fortune what she remembered of the tropical place she came from. Mary felt sick and annoyed and clenched her fists that she would never be able to do so.

'Miss Mary, you're safe.'

She looked at Fortune's doll, remembering how the one she was given protected her that day in the museum. Mary was sure that it did. Why, she could not say, only that it did. But why did this one not protect Fortune? How dare they hurt the girl! And for what? If Mrs Denbie were standing in front of her, she would… she would… She ground her teeth in anger.

'Miss Mary!' the voice insisted.

The scent of violets coloured the air. It brought with it visions of a small girl, dishevelled, her hair unkempt, nightdress muddy and arms bruised, standing beside her. Mary felt tormented. It was getting nearer to the time she was dreading. She so wished she could quiet her mind. But first, she must go and collect Cook, then together they would set out for the morgue. She must be strong.

'Miss Mary!' the voice shouted in annoyance. Mary was aware of someone tugging at her dress. She looked down, startled.

'Well, answer her,' Archie said from behind. Mary turned towards him, her thoughts broken. 'Answer her!' he insisted.

Archie was standing in the middle of the room. He was smiling. Constable O'Connor was smiling. Lestrade too. She was confused. Her eyes dropped down. Fortune was looking up, also smiling. Mary's mouth fell open, her eyes widened and she started in fright.

'Are you real?' Mary reached down and felt the girl's face. It was soft and warm. She drew her fingers back in surprise and gazed towards Archie.

'You ain't seeing things,' he said.

Mary fell on to her knees and grasped the girl and hugged her tightly.

'You're real!' she shouted. 'You're alive! Archie, Fortune's alive. She's not dead.'

'Me not dead, Miss Mary,' Fortune said and then giggled. 'Did you think I was a Jumbie?'

A rush of relief washed over Mary and she stuttered and mumbled as she held on to the small girl.

'I found her in the basement,' O'Connor said. 'She was tied up and gagged. But the clever thing had already worked through some of the ropes.'

'Constable O'Connor!' Mary shouted, unable to quiet her joy.

'She's got a tale to tell, all right,' O'Connor said.

'That Mrs Denbie is the Grey Lady,' Fortune said triumphantly. 'I saw her. But she grabbed me when I catch her up in the park. Miss Mary, she and her sister put a bag on my head and tied me up.'

'Sister? Don't you mean her daughter?'

'No, Miss Mary, not Miss Lorna. Her sister.'

Mary looked over to Archie. 'The Denbies' maid!' Her face contorted with the realisation. 'They're sisters!

How stupid of me—why else would she be in the photographs?' Mary turned to Fortune. 'But why ain't you dead?'

'Well,' O'Connor said quietly. He glanced over his shoulder to make sure Lestrade was not nearby, but the Inspector had left the room. 'As I gather from what everyone's said, I reckon since no one can prove that Mrs Denbie murdered those men, it's all circumstantial, after all, then murdering Fortune would be a mistake, especially if they did it back in Holland Park. If it were ever discovered she was the Grey Lady, then it'd be easy enough to know who killed the child.

'But they couldn't take her with them to do it later, not a screaming, kicking girl, or even one asleep, not out on to the streets and into a cab at such short notice and risk anyone seeing.' He shook his head. 'She's lucky she's so noticeable.' He pinched Fortune's cheek. 'This little scallywag would be easily identified by anyone who saw her and the street was still busy after what had happened. They had to leave their big trunk behind, otherwise she might be in it. So, they left her tied up instead while they scarpered.'

Again, he looked over his shoulders, Inspector Lestrade was in the back bedroom.

'And when they brought her here, I reckon the cabbie was someone they knew and trusted…'

Mary understood, they could not take the time to find the cabbie, to take Fortune away with them.

'You know, you ain't half clever, *Sergeant* O'Con-nor,' Mary said. Suddenly her mouth dropped open. The smile left her lips and she went quite pale. 'Oh! Dear me!' she gasped, staggering back and flopping on to the sofa.

'Miss Mary?' Fortune said and grasped her hands.

'What is it?' Archie asked.

'That poor girl,' she whispered. 'The one who died in the river, the one we thought was Fortune. I was so happy that Fortune is alive, I'd forgotten about her. God forgive me for forgetting! She was someone else's child, Archie.'

Mary clutched Fortune, happy she was alive, while her heart grieved for the young girl lying in Charing Cross morgue.

28

ONE LAST THROW OF
THE DICE

LESTRADE DELAYED his interrogation of the maid. He knew there was little she could tell him that he did not know already. The Denbies would try to flee the country; his first duty, therefore, was to inform the port authorities to be on the lookout. Sadly, there was a new investigation to conduct: the murder of the poor girl mistaken for Fortune.

Because of that, Mary's happiness was tempered with a heavy heart. Her relief that Fortune was alive, though, was evident. On their way to Baker Street, Mary kept leaning across to give Fortune big, silent hugs, much to the maid's embarrassment. However, Mary's sense of foreboding refused to leave. Her fingers were drumming again.

Archie, clearly knew what that meant.

Mary sighed.

'That snipe knew of the Denbies' trick,' she said. 'Lestrade wasn't listening to me. Hawthorne's mixed up in all of this. I just can't figure out how.'

'But you've got an idea.'

'A crazy one. I just need to think it through.'

They dropped Archie off at the Dibbles' pie shop and left for Holland Park. By the time they arrived at the Rose Garden, there was a wicked grin on Mary's face. The further they went from the Denbies' flat, and the nearer to home, the happier she became. She would worry about Hawthorne later, but for now, she was content with the moment.

As yet, Cook did not realise the maid was alive, and knowing her aversion to ghost stories, Mary leant over and whispered conspiratorially to Fortune, a mischievous thought having entered her mind.

'Listen, I'm going to go in first,' she could barely conceal a giggle. 'I'm going to look all glum and afraid and tell Cook she needs to get ready so we can go to Charing Cross—'

'Miss Mary?' Fortune gave her a puzzled look.

'Now, after a few minutes, you come in with your arms outstretched and your eyes closed, moaning and wailing like a ghost, you know—'

'Miss Mary?'

'Ooooooh! Ooooooh! Say, you're here to haunt her for always telling you off.' Mary giggled.

'No, Miss Mary, I can't do that,' Fortune said. 'Cook

will think I'm a Jumbie and faint and die. And then she'll come back and haunt me.'

Mary sniggered. Fortune looked miffed. Mary grinned and nudged the small girl with her elbow. An impish smile cut across Fortune's face, and they quickly fell into a whispered conversation.

The house stood quiet in the afternoon sun. Mary stared at it and thought it looked different with the knowledge that the maid was alive. Like cat burglars, she and Fortune crept around to the back door, avoiding any windows on the way, the devilish grin not leaving Mary's lips. Her heart fluttered with joy.

She could already hear Cook scolding her for playing such a trick while hugging the maid, laughing and crying at the same time.

The back door to the kitchen, as usual, was open, left ajar to let out the hot air and steam from the cooking. Mary peeped in. She expected to see Cook at the stove or the table, peeling or kneading, busy with something, but the room was empty. The dirty dishes from lunch should be piled beside the sink. Yet there were none, the draining board was bare. Two pots bubbled noisily on the stove. On the floor was a clatter of wooden spoons and crockery. A chair was overturned. A glass shattered; the shards glittering on the floor.

A cold hand of dread gripped Mary's throat. It tingled her fingers and rippled across the hairs of her skin.

Holding her panic in check, she lifted the pots from

the fire. The handles were baking and she almost dropped them; the contents had nearly evaporated. A trickle of sweat ran down her cheek. Now that the noisy bubbling pots was taken away from the flame, the whole house was silent.

She listened. All she could hear was the drumming of her heart.

At that moment, Fortune came in, arms outstretched and eyes closed. A wail was about to erupt from her laughing lips. Mary quickly placed a hand across the girl's mouth.

'Something's wrong,' she whispered. 'I don't like this.' Mary looked around. 'I don't like this one bit.' Fortune looked confused as Mary led her to the pantry. 'I want you to hide in here until I find out what's going on.'

She opened the door and pushed the maid in. There was a loud gasp; she felt the small girl flinch and shy back into her.

Cook was lying on the pantry floor. Mary rushed over to her. To her relief, Cook was only unconscious. There was a bruise on the side of her face. Mary pulled Fortune over. She could see she was frightened.

'I want you to close the door and stay with her.' But Fortune's eyes were wide with terror. 'Cook needs you. You'll look after her for me—yes?' The small girl crouched next to Cook, she wrapped her arms around her legs, shivering. She nodded. 'Now, don't make a sound.'

Mary edged out of the pantry. As she left the kitchen,

she picked up an iron poker. She crept along the hallway towards the dining room. The table was prepared for lunch, with dishes and cutlery neatly laid out. She tiptoed to the drawing room and slipped in. It too was empty. She heard muffled sounds: an argument from the floor above.

Quieting her panic, Mary slipped out into the corridor and jumped in fright.

Mrs Denbie lay sprawled like some twisted mannequin across the bottom treads of the stairs. She was wearing the grey dress, the one with the torn hem. A wave of nausea tightened Mary's stomach when she realised the woman was dead.

Mrs Denbie's veil was pulled back. A white sack-like mask was half on and half off her face. Where the eyes should be, there were two glass-covered holes. A tube connected the mask to a small bag by Mrs Denbie's chest. The device she wore looked like the drawing of Selwin Barnet's rebreathing apparatus Mary had seen in the newspaper. The cutting still lay on her bed in the attic.

Mary glanced up the stairs nervously and realised that Mrs Denbie must have fallen down them.

The argument started up again. It was coming from Mrs Grady's room, she thought, and Mary's skin prickled. She swallowed her fears and placed a foot on the first tread and crept up the stairs, gripping the poker tightly. It felt weighty in her shaking hand. Raising it higher, she slipped into her mistress's room through the open door.

A fight had strewn the carpet with crockery, books, gowns and shoes. The sheets were hanging off the bed. To Mary's surprise, Hawthorne was rising from the floor. A trickle of blood ran down his face. The pieces of a shattered jug crunched under his foot as he tottered upright.

His eyes alighted on Mary and he tensed in recognition.

'What're you doing here?' Mary screwed up her mouth and menaced the fire-iron into his face.

Suddenly, he flew at her. Mary fell back in surprise. He grasped her arm and twisted it. She screamed and instinctively kicked out and heard him grunt in pain. He swung her around and flung her across the room. As Mary tumbled away, she thrashed the poker in a wild arc and heard a dull thwack and another cry of pain. The throw sent her sprawling over and across the bed.

She was quickly up, ready for his next attack. The lawyer, though, was clutching his shoulder and hopping on one foot. Then a gunshot shattered the air. He glanced towards the sound in horror and dashed out of the door.

Mary rushed after him. Hawthorne was hurrying down the stairs when yet another gunshot exploded from further along the corridor in Ella's room. Mary froze. The shouting started once more. This time, she recognised Mr Venables's voice.

With small, hesitant steps, she edged to Ella's bedroom door and listened. Her mind was numb. She took a deep breath. Raising the poker high, Mary grasped the handle, turned it sharply and rushed in.

Almost immediately, she stopped.

Pressed against the wall at the back of the room was Mrs Denbie's father. His face was drenched in sweat; the front of his suit ran wet with blood. One hand was around Mrs Grady's waist; she was almost unconscious, and he was holding her upright. His other hand held a blade. His eyes gazed unerringly at Mr Venables.

Crouched in a corner, the Butler held the wrist of Lorna Denbie with a firm grip. In his other hand, he steadied a revolver that was aimed at the old man. Blood oozed from the Butler's waist and he grimaced in pain.

The girl was clearly terrified. She squirmed and cried and tried to pull free, but the Butler held her tightly. Mary noticed that her alabaster complexion was no more than make-up; the white powder was streaked with her tears, revealing the true colour of her flesh beneath it. The dark circle of her eyes was mascara that ran in grey-black smudges down her cheeks.

Mary shook. There was a cold determination in both men's eyes. Both burned with anger and hatred of the other.

29

JOSHUA SMITH

'COME NO CLOSER, CHILD,' the old man warned. He struggled to hold Mrs Grady upright. 'My business isn't concluded yet.'

Mary stood half in and half out of the room. Although she willed her legs to move, they would not budge an inch.

'Well, Tobias,' the old man said to Mr Venables, 'it looks like you've done for me all right. I'm leaking like a sieve. I think you've killed me, man.' He gave a low laugh. 'So make up your mind, because I've not long for this world. My granddaughter's freedom for Rosie's life —it's an honest enough bargain.'

Mr Venables gripped Lorna Denbie's hand and twisted her wrist until the girl, wincing in pain. He raised his gun, extending his arm towards her grandfather.

'Think about it, Tobias,' the old man cautioned and

hid his face in Mrs Grady's hair. 'You miss and she's dead. Even if you don't, I might still kill her. Think about it, man.' He held the knife firmly against Mrs Grady.

'I could let you bleed to death,' Mr Venables said angrily and the old man laughed.

'I'll do that soon enough, Tobias, but Rosie will come with me before then.' There resided a grim determination in the old man's eyes that said he would not be denied.

'I warn you, Joshua Smith—'

'No, no, Tobias. No more threats,' Mr Smith said wearily. 'I reckon it's too late for any more of those from either of us. The stakes are on the table; we play the hands we're dealt. It's time to choose.'

The room fell quiet. In the heavy silence, Mary's mind swirled. She remembered the photograph in Mr Smith's room. She was now certain—the neatly dressed man with the white hair was Mr Venables. No doubt Patrick Grady was one of the others on the quayside, under the prow of the *Jane Rose*. And Joshua Smith knew Rose Grady.

'Well?' Mr Smith asked. His voice was a whisper.

'How do I know you'll keep your part of the bargain?'

'My word will have to be good enough, Tobias. We can hardly take the time to draw up a contract. And I'm not sure my lawyer would be up to it after Rosie crowned him.'

'Let her go, Mr Venables.' The sound of her voice

surprised Mary. If Lorna's freedom would guarantee Mrs Grady's life, she for one was willing to accept the bargain.

'Well?' Mr Smith asked again.

The Butler hesitated. Mary could see the doubts in his eyes. There was fear there also. Mr Smith, however, was cold and single-minded.

'Please, Mr Venables,' Mary said.

'I've lost the game, Tobias. Listen to the girl. I'll salvage this or nothing at all. I'll make a deal with the devil for Lorna's freedom. And I'll keep my part.'

The girl squirmed, her eyes closed, she was trembling as she cried.

'Please, Mr Venables,' she whimpered, 'spare my grandfather.'

'Come on, man, make your mind up. Time's not on either of our sides,' Mr Smith said.

'What choice is there?' Mary asked.

'Aye, Tobias, listen to the child.'

Still Mr Venables hesitated. He looked as if he was fighting with some demon. His face scowled and twitched as something passed through his mind and he gave a low snarl of resignation.

With some reluctance, the Butler released his grip, and Lorna pulled her hand free and rubbed life back into the numb wrist. The gun, though, was still levelled on her grandfather. She glanced hesitantly at the Butler, as if unsure of his intentions, and then began to edge away, testing him. She looked at her grandfather, and Mary saw the old man smile and nod his head.

'Get off with you, Lorna,' Mr Smith said. Lorna gazed at him in uncertainty. 'Go with your mother and tell her I love her.'

'But Mrs Denbie is dead,' Mary said.

The old man scowled and whispered under his breath, 'Frances, her aunt, is dead, girl. My other daughter is her mother.'

'The maid, you mean?'

He nodded.

'Frances underestimated the old girl's strength.' He lifted up Mrs Grady's head, a rueful grin washed across his face. 'As did that damn lawyer, when she smashed him with a vase and pushed her over the bannister. It was my fault, all my fault to let it go that far.'

'Granddad…' Lorna dithered, reluctant to leave, but Mr Smith smiled at her kindly. He gathered up his strength and a softness came to his eyes.

'Go, Lorna,' he said quietly. 'You can't stay and I can't leave and that's the way of it. A bargain's a bargain, is it not, Tobias? I'll keep mine even if Patrick Grady never kept his.'

Lorna paused.

'He won't shoot,' Mary said, but more to Mr Venables than the frightened girl.

Mr Smith did not speak, but his eyes seemed to say goodbye. With reluctance, Lorna began to leave, and then she stopped beside Mary. A frightened look came to her face.

'I did not lie,' she said. 'He is alive.'

'Who?' Mary asked.

'Your brother is in great danger. Trouble surrounds him like a mist. I do not understand it—your brother is both a lie and a truth at the same time. I cannot explain that. But he has embarked on a dangerous journey. It is something—' Mary scowled her loathing of Lorna's visions. 'You do not believe, I can see that. I can understand. Forgive me my deception of your mistress. But I have not deceived you.'

Lorna Denbie took one last look at her grandfather and left. The clatter of her footsteps echoed along the corridor, disappeared down the stairs and across the entrance hall. They heard the front door slam, and then no more.

A hush descended and gripped the room. No one moved or made a sound as several minutes passed. A calm settled on Mary. She could hear her thoughts again. She lowered the poker, realising she was still brandishing it and, for some reason, it made her feel very foolish.

'I've kept my part, Joshua, now you keep yours,' Mr Venables said.

'In time, Tobias, in time,' Joshua Smith said softly. 'Let's talk a little first and give Lorna half an hour. That will suffice. I reckon that's all I have left in me as it is.'

Mr Smith wiped the sweat from his face with his sleeve. He turned his eyes to Mary.

'Lorna speaks the truth about your brother. Aye, most of what we did was trickery, but even so, she has the power. Whatever vision she had of your brother affected her that day you came to visit us. It took her by surprise. She did not lie to you.'

'I'm expected to believe that, am I?'

Mr Smith nodded his head, understanding her doubts.

'There's far too much water under the bridge, and that's for sure. Aye, I know we tried to trick you at the time and I know I can't convince you. Lorna is gifted, that at least is true. So I'll say it again, for what it is worth: she spoke the truth about your brother. She could never control her visions, and every now and then, she sees things in the mist and there is no trickery involved.'

'A curse? Nefrusheri? The Grey Lady? Was all that true? That powder that made us see things?'

'As I said, much of what we did was trickery. But take it or leave it as you want.' Mr Smith winced in pain and the hand that held the knife shook.

'I'll tend your wound if you'll let Mrs Grady go,' Mary said.

Mr Smith's eyes came up to meet hers.

'I think you would as well. I shall release her in a while, child. But I'll not be saved for the hangman,' and he dipped his head politely as if to say thanks. 'So,

Tobias, I see you've done well for yourself. Lower the gun, man, it's done—I'll keep my promise.'

'I thought you were dead,' the Butler said and did as he was asked.

'Along with Patrick Grady in that cursed ship. Aye, well, that is not surprising.'

'You were all friends?' Mary asked.

'Joshua Smith at your service, Miss Finch,' the old man said politely, 'First Mate and only survivor of the *Jane Rose*. A heathen ship with a heathen cargo, a heathen crew and a heathen captain. A green crew of adventurers made up of few that never sailed needs a good First Mate.' He nodded. 'Lorna will have found a hansom by now, I reckon, and be heading to find her mother,' he said quietly, almost to himself.

He closed his eyes, and Mary imagined him seeing his one remaining daughter in his mind's eye.

30

A DEATH IN THE ROSE GARDEN

'It was to be my last trip, Miss Finch, that cursed journey on the *Jane Rose*. I would retire in some style to a farm I bought in Virginia with my wife and daughters, and forget about Patrick Grady and his cheating ways. Because a cheat he was.'

He turned his gaze towards Mr Venables.

'You did not know, did you, Tobias? He planned to have me arrested once we landed, on a trumped-up charge of murder, so he could steal my share of the profits. But fate decided otherwise. First a wrecking and then a civil war in which I lost everything, including my wife and my property. Never was a man so prone to ill luck.'

'The same luck as your cargo would have brought?' Mary said bitterly, suspecting that it was guns they carried, but fearing that it could have been worse.

Smith did not answer. Whether he felt remorse or pity

for his deeds, she did not know. But she wondered if Lorna Denbie understood her words, or knew about the misery her grandfather's cargo would bring, when she so vividly described the crew's fate. Did her grandfather tell her? Were they his words she spoke, so carefully rehearsed?

'When did Patrick ever cheat you?' Mr Venables asked.

'Patrick Grady cheated everyone—even Siobhan. He left her and his child to die in penury when he could have saved them.'

'She's dead? Siobhan is dead?' Mary asked.

'He had money,' Smith said ignoring Mary. 'He made vows that he conveniently forgot and allowed my cousin to starve to death.'

'You and Siobhan are—'

'Cousins,' Mr Venables answered Mary's question. 'But no love was lost there, Joshua, as I remember it.'

'She was blood, nevertheless. And you forget I knew Patrick Grady well. Cheating was his stock-in-trade. That's how he lived his life. He was no plaster saint, no matter what he wanted everyone to believe. He didn't expect Siobhan to be disinherited, though. He didn't expect to lose all the Fitzwilliam gold. Then he no longer needed her. Why do you think he divorced her?''

'You know that's not true,' Mr Venables said. 'He was in jail, and she was abandoned by you and your kin. That's why he agreed to the divorce—so she could go

back to her family. She would have starved otherwise—
the little you cared.'

'I know the truth!' Smith said angrily. 'I know what
he did!'

'This charade is all about revenge?' Mary said.

'This is not a game,' Smith barked. 'There was a debt
to be paid and money to be returned, stolen from me by
that devil.'

'And there's the truth, Mary,' Mr Venables said curtly.
'This is about greed and no more. But why now? It's
been over thirty years since the *Jane Rose* sank?'

Smith winced. His pain called him back to the present
and he ground his teeth in anger.

'Such ill-luck,' he said in a hoarse whisper. 'None of
this would have happened had we not come back to
England. Only Frances's act was given a touring engagement across Europe. In truth, I had not even thought of
that devil in all those years until I found out how well
Rose done out of my money. She had all those years of
living like royalty, while I struggled. I wanted to see her
brought low as I was once.'

'Did you plan to kill her as well?' Mary asked.

Smith gazed up to the ceiling. 'We were never going
to kill Rosie. That would not do. Just steal her money and
leave her in the poorhouse for the rest of her life. A taste
of what I have endured.'

'But the laudanum?'

'That was a mistake.' He shook his head. 'That was

Frances forgetting the plan and that greedy lawyer wanting her dead so she couldn't contest his writ. That's when it all went wrong,' he said angrily. 'Nor was any harm meant to the little girl.'

Mary sneered—she knew better. Fortune was lucky and no more. Had Smith's scheme succeeded, she would have disappeared, her body never to be found, of that Mary was certain. But finally, she understood their plans.

'You just wanted to drive Mrs Grady out of her mind,' she said. 'The fake séance, the visions, the curse of the Grey Lady—you made it all seem real by killing those men.'

'We killed no one,' Smith said. 'Their imaginations did that.'

'Do you really believe that, Mr Smith?' Mary asked. But he would not answer. 'Asking for no more money than your consultation fees was a ploy. That way, Mrs Grady would not think you cheats. The real money would come from the will.'

'You're a clever girl,' Smith said. 'What else do you know?'

'That all the insights Lorna had must have come from you.'

Smith placed his head against the wall and closed his eyes. He did not answer.

'I saw the photograph of you beside the *Jane Rose*. I think Mr Venables was with you on the quayside. I'm guessing it was a long journey across the Atlantic.'

'Aye, it was that.' Smith smiled. 'Things are said of a personal nature when the nights are long. Yes, Patrick told me many things on many such nights. His name for Rosie, where they met, that song; many more things that Lorna would have revealed over the coming weeks, but for that snipe's interference.'

'No doubt you had an accomplice in Professor Cavendish's expedition,' Mary said. 'How else could you know about the Grey Lady so quickly? Did he send you a telegram before he died?'

'His death was an accident. The curse, though, was a bonus. But I think you've guessed that. Now, you tell the rest, girl,' Smith said, looking at Mr Venables rather than Mary.

'You wanted to drive Mrs Grady out of her mind, playing with her hopes of speaking to the dead. You saw your chance when you found out about the expedition. After all, it was easy to convince everyone of Lorna's credibility by using that powder on us.'

'Powder?' Mr Venables asked.

'Something I picked up in Africa,' Smith said.

'Lestrade called it a hallucinogenic. I remembered the smell of violets each time it was used. Why did it not affect Lorna and Mrs Denbie at the séance?'

'Oh! It did,' Smith said. 'But you become accustomed after a while and have some control of the visions.'

'And Mrs Denbie—or whatever her name was—wore the underwater device when posing as the Grey Lady.'

Mary fell quiet for a few moments, deep in thought. 'Then there's Hawthorne's part—some more misery to heap upon the old lady. That was how you planned to get Mrs Grady's money. Siobhan *is* dead, just like Cook remembered. Did Hawthorne find someone to impersonate her? Did he fabricate a will? I imagine that during the famine, records were seldom updated.'

Smith was almost encouraging her to speak with his smiles and nods.

'Then what would happen? Would the mysterious Siobhan Grady, formally Fitzwilliam, die and leave all her worldly possession to… who? Her surviving kin? Your children and grandchild? And, of course, you could not show yourself in case Mr Venables recognised you.'

Smith rallied, took some deep breaths. His side was quite wet with his blood.

'We would have claimed the inheritance from abroad, somewhere lacking British justice and scrutiny,' he said. 'I'm letting you know this, Tobias, so we can come to an understanding. You are to leave Lorna alone. None of you are to go after her, or plot against her, do you hear? She's free, and I want her to stay free. Say whatever you want to the police, but keep her out of it. You can blame Frances and me, and you won't be telling any lies. In truth, all Lorna did was act her role, to convince Rosie of the things she spoke about.'

'She's as guilty as you are in the eyes of the law,' Mr Venables said ruefully.

'Perhaps that is so, Tobias. I know the law will seek her, but you don't have to help them.' He looked up at the Butler with uncertain eyes. 'I do not have a right to ask, but I do. She'll not trouble you or Rosie again. Her mother will see to that. Anne wanted nothing to do with this. I am the true culprit. I'm sure you could convince the law of that.'

'You ask for my charity.'

'You will never see the child again,' Smith said.

The Butler was silent for a few moments. Whatever thoughts came to mind made him curl his lips in disgust. And then give a slight nod.

Smith sighed and took a deep breath. His whisper was just audible.

'I'll say it again, Miss Finch, even if you don't believe me. Lorna saw the truth concerning your brother. I'll not try to convince you more, only to say I have nothing to gain from lies now. Take it or leave it.'

His gaze became distant; it was as if his eyes were with his granddaughter wherever she was. Then his fingers opened and the knife slipped free.

Time seemed to slow and stutter. Only the singing of the birds from outside released it to move on once more. Joshua Smith lay propped against the wall, quietly still.

By time the police mobilised, Lorna Denbie and her mother would be gone, faded away into the crowds. Before the week was out, they would be off under false names, on the continent, or in Ireland, or on a ship bound for the Americas or South Africa. Mary had no doubt of Joshua Smith's efficiency: he would have made plans for their escape should there be a disaster.

She understood now. When she and Archie broke into his flat, Smith had to act fast and recklessly. This was his one last throw of the dice. Had he succeeded, it would have been Mrs Grady's body lying at the bottom of the stairs, her death caused by accident or suicide brought on by guilt or nervousness or just madness. And since she had no relatives, no one would have contested the will held by Siobhan Grady, risen from the dead to claim her inheritance.

Mr Venables stood shakily and clutched his bleeding side. Mary helped him carry Mrs Grady over to Ella's bed.

'He spoke the truth in parts,' the Butler said. 'We were friends once. For that friendship, at least, I owe him my silence, and no more.'

If there was charity in allowing Lorna Denbie to escape, Mary did not know or understand. For the moment, she did not care. She ran for the doctor.

31

MARY'S LOCKET SPEAKS

FOR SEVERAL DAYS, a conspiracy of silence dominated the Rose Garden. Mrs Grady took to her bed on her doctor's insistence. Ella and Fortune haunted the corridors. Mary did not know whom to speak to, so it seemed sensible to remain quiet, especially as Cook and Mr Venables kept their counsel.

But eventually her curiosity got the better of her and she asked Mr Venables, was it he in the picture by Smith's bedside?

'Aye,' Mr Venables said. A darkness entered his eyes and a sadness came to his face that he could not hide. 'I have done many things I am not proud of, Mary. One was to have helped finance Patrick Grady's purchase of the *Jane Rose* knowing full well the despicable use he would make of it. For that I have paid in ways I care not to speak of. For that I will be judged when my time comes. Until then, let sleeping dogs lie.'

He did not elaborate and Mary could only guess at Patrick Grady's sins.

Having questioned everyone at the Rose Garden, some days later, Inspector Lestrade returned to inform them that Fogarty Hawthorne had been apprehended trying to flee the country, and that the coming inquest would more than likely acquit the Butler and Mrs Grady as they acted in self-defence. Hawthorne's part was more of a tangled web that would take time to unravel.

But Lestrade was confused as to the whereabouts of Lorna Denbie. Mr Venables's account of the day she disappeared challenged Hawthorne's.

'I don't understand it, Miss Finch,' Lestrade said as she walked him to his carriage. 'Why would Mr Hawthorne get that one fact wrong? You were there: was Lorna Denbie in the house or not? Did you not see her?'

'I saw only what Mr Venables saw, Inspector,' she said and left it at that.

'Well, she and the maid are gone,' Lestrade said dejectedly. 'Vanished into thin air—now there's a trick if ever I saw one.'

Mary considered it a good thing that Hawthorne did not know all that Joshua Smith knew. At least Mrs Grady could keep some of her secrets and the dead could rest in peace.

On Sunday morning, as Mary lay in bed, Lorna Denbie's parting words returned to nag her. She awoke from a dream in which Danny Finch was falling, and she could not stop him. Even though she reached out her hand, his fingers slipped through hers and he was gone.

She lay staring at the ceiling. Unable to sleep, she arose, went downstairs with the intention of stepping outside for some air. To her surprise, Ella and Fortune were lying against each other, curled up under a single blanket by Mrs Grady's bedroom door. Both were asleep on the rug outside the room like faithful lapdogs guarding their mistress. Oscar was snuggled up warmly between them. She wondered if they had done this every night since the fearful day that Joshua Smith died.

She lifted Ella and took her to her room and tucked her into bed. The cat followed and leapt effortlessly up to slip beside the sleeping girl. When Mary returned, Fortune was awake, leaning against the door and yawning, rubbing her knuckles into her eyes.

'Will Mistress be all right, Miss Mary?' she asked.

'Of course, she will,' Mary said, though her voice sounded hollow. She reached down a hand.

'Will that other lady be our mistress?'

'Listening at keyholes?' Mary smiled and the young girl's head drooped.

'Jumb—'

'Sh-shhh!' whispered Mary. 'No more talk about ghosts or spirits. Mrs Grady is the mistress and no one else. Bed for you. You've got a busy morning—lighting the fires, getting hot water on, a bit of cleaning. I'll give you a hand and we'll get it done, just like that,' and she snapped her fingers. 'Then you can accompany the mistress to church, if she's up for it.'

'Ain't you going to come as well?'

'No, Fortune, I've got a few things to do first.'

THAT MORNING, MARY WENT TO BAKER STREET. SHE was about to knock on the door of 221b when it suddenly opened.

'Hello, Dr Watson,' she said. 'Is Mr Holmes in, by any chance?'

'I am afraid you've missed him, Mary. He left for Shropshire earlier this morning—hot on the heels of a murderer with Inspector Lestrade in tow.'

'You did not go with him?'

'Alas, no. I have some pressing business to which I must attend. Walk with me, perhaps I can be of assistance.'

'Oh, I just wanted to talk through what has happened recently.'

They set out in a leisurely walk towards Regent's Park.

'I thought that might be your mission,' Dr Watson said. 'I took the opportunity to present the facts, as told to me by Archie, to Holmes some nights ago—I hope you do not mind my presumption.' Mary shook her head. 'He agreed with your conclusions.'

Dr Watson nodded his in admiration, but Mary wondered if it was because of her conclusions or Joshua Smith's audacious plan.

'Holmes made an enquiry. A telegram was sent to Mr Smith from Egypt. Like you, he surmised it probably detailed the curse on the tomb, and that gave Smith the idea. Smith no doubt suspected something of the sort would be discovered. This *game* was long in the planning, it seems, to have an accomplice attached to the expedition. The use of a drug was a novelty that Mr Holmes has decided to investigate further. He was disappointed there was not a sample he could analyse. Now, what is it you really want to know?'

'My locket, Dr Watson. Lorna Denbie's knowledge was intimate.'

'Ah! The locket,' Dr Watson gave a low laugh. 'You want to know if Lorna Denbie possesses any supernatural powers.'

The doctor stopped and his face took on a thoughtful look.

'I will tell you what Holmes did—or rather, made me do. *"Watson,"* he said, *"you know my methods, apply them!"''*

Dr Watson took the locket and held it in his palm.

'That it is only a half suggests that there must be another half. It has clearly been broken by being worked back and forth, and that took patience and effort. That means it was important that it should be divided. It is made of finely crafted gold, so who it was that broke it did not mind ruining such a beautiful object.

'That your part of the locket contains half a picture, that of a boy, suggests that the other part must contain the other half of the picture, more than likely of a girl—you, Mary. A relationship is inferred. In all likelihood, Holmes reasoned, the locket was divided to ensure each recipient, should they be removed from each other's company, would still be aware of the other.

'And you wear the locket with pride—why else wear a broken object?

'That you are searching for the person whose picture it contains, or are likely to search for him, can be assumed and played with by an experienced confidence trickster, used to reading the slight nuances in a face or the expressions in a sentence. Someone like Lorna Denbie—quick witted with skills honed from years of performing her mind reading-tricks.'

Mary nodded. Lorna Denbie was like Mr Holmes in that respect, she thought, her mind attuned to such trivialities.

'As for the blood in Lorna Denbie's hand, Holmes says it was a simple enough ruse—merely a crushed pellet, the type actors use when on stage, the container wiped away by Mrs Denbie when she mopped her daughter's palm.'

Mary sighed. 'Of course. I fear I shall never be up to Mr Holmes's standard. How could I have missed such a simple trick?'

'Ah! Well, for once, I can answer that. It was personal, Mary. We are all biased, and sometimes that means we fail to see the obvious. Even Holmes has fallen into such traps. But he has the unique ability to step outside of his body and view himself as another entity. If it were someone else's locket, Mary, your keen wit would have penetrated the confidence trick quickly, I have no doubt of that.'

When they reached the end of Baker Street, Mary turned to go.

'You will continue your search for your brother, nevertheless?' Dr Watson enquired.

'I will,' Mary said, 'starting today.'

32

DANIEL FINCH IS ON
THE RUN

MRS FORTESQUE WAS as Mary remembered her: a pinched-faced lady with a hard, severe, admonishing expression. They glowered at each other. Her former employer was just about to raise her hand to smack her runaway maid when the woman spied Archie.

The boy, whose legs had recovered sufficiently, stood beside Mary, menacingly broad-shouldered. His eyes narrowed, he puffed his chest out and he gave Mrs Fortesque a deep, penetrating stare of dislike. He appeared so threatening that the lady stepped back and clutched the doorframe tightly.

When Mary asked how she came to employ her, Mrs Fortesque almost spat out the words.

'Mrs Chidewell, Chillwell—something like that— brought you here. I don't know where she lives. Across the river—Southwark way, near the cathedral.' She scowled at Mary. 'I could have you arrested.'

'What for? Running away from an old cow, like you?' Mary mocked. 'I ain't your property.'

Mrs Fortesque sniffed and slammed the door shut.

<hr>

Some hours later, Mary and Archie were wandering the streets around Southwark Cathedral. She had a vague memory of a house with a green door, and an equally vague recollection of her aunt's face and the names of her children. Only when she stood outside number twelve, which did indeed have a green door, did the fog in her mind lift and she knew where she was.

She was happy here once, she remembered, and her resentment at being sent away years ago came flooding back. As she stood there, she wondered how she would feel to see Mrs Chidewell again, even knowing that what had been done, would have been done with a good reason.

A tall boy of about seventeen answered her knock, and led Mary and Archie into the front room. An ailing woman sat on a tacky sofa. Mary recognised her immediately.

'Aunt Grace,' murmured Mary.

'Mary Finch, as I live and breathe,' Grace Chidewell

coughed. 'Chas, tell Jenny to bring some tea. You'll take some tea, won't you, Mary? Say you will, won't you?'

'Of course, Auntie,' Mary said looking around the room. It had not changed one bit in three years, only a little more faded than she recalled. There was sadness in Mrs Chidewell's eyes that made Mary sit quietly and listen as the woman explained why she sent her away. She had not intended to ask, but was grateful to be told.

'I never wanted to let you go, Mary. But you was old enough to work, so I found you a position I thought suitable. Things were hard at that time. Charlie senior was out of work, and apart from Chas and Fawn, the kids were too young.'

'She moped for a good month,' Chas said.

'A good month,' Grace confirmed. 'I should have come a visiting, but my health was never that good and I couldn't bring myself to do so. Forgive me, Mary, but I really couldn't. It would have broken my heart to see your little face. But I wrote to you and was sad you never wrote back. Why didn't you write back, Mary? Was you that angry that you couldn't answer my letters?'

'Letters, Auntie? But I never got any letters.'

'But I wrote, Mary. Telling you to keep up your writing and reading and how we were doing and asking how you was doing. And when things got better again, I told you that we would have you back, if you wanted to come. But you never did once reply.'

Mary grimaced—so the Fortesques had taken her letters amongst everything else.

'I even sent Chas around, I was so worried.'

'Some old bat said you were happy there and you didn't want to leave,' Chas said. 'I come around a couple more times, but she said you were out in school each time.'

Mary told them of the awful time she had with Mrs Fortesque. How she'd run away and worked for the Grimwigs, and now for Mrs Grady. As for school—Mary laughed. At least the 'old bat' had plenty of newspapers, so she did keep up with her reading. She saw the worry crease Grace's face and the sadness of her neglect hidden there.

'What happened, Auntie, happened,' Mary said, practically. 'I was angry, I'll admit—but I understand now.'

'I'm not really your aunt, Mary,' Grace said. 'Not blood, anyway. I was your mum's friend. I took you in after your parents died, after the accident.'

'Accident?' Mary said.

'Bless me, you don't remember, do you? Oh! You were so young. Here, Jenny, go and get me box of photographs. Your family was coming back on the river from Chatham, Mary, where your dad had just found a job. The boat collided with another in the fog and lots of people drowned—your mum and dad didn't make it. It was Danny who rescued you, holding on to you until you was safe. Afterwards, you cried and cried; you just wanted your mum and dad. That broke my heart, that did.' Grace mopped a tear from her eye when she told Mary where her parent's were buried.

'I'm ever so grateful, Auntie. God knows I am,' Mary said. 'You've told me more about Mum and Dad than I ever knew before. But where's Danny? Do you know?'

'Mr Fuller took him. He was a friend of your father. We sort of had to split you up because neither of us could take you both. I was the one who snapped the locket in two,' Grace said. 'It was the only thing I could think to do so as you'd both could have a piece of your parents, as it were. The Fullers lived over in Gravesend, but then something awful happened.'

Grace hesitated and chewed her lower lip.

'Him and his wife were murdered. It was in the papers,' Chas said sheepishly.

'What is the matter?' Mary asked.

'Oh! Just—' and Chas shook his head sadly. 'The coppers were looking for the boy living with them. That'd be Danny. They wanted to question him. He vanished soon after their deaths. It don't mean anything, Mary,' Chas said quickly. 'It's just what they do. Question everyone.'

'Did they think he had something to do with the murders?'

Chas shrugged. 'When Danny vanished, that was suspicious, they said. They thought he might have been dead as well, but he ain't. I seen him about a month ago, up west ways.'

Mary leant closer.

'Near Putney, by Barnes, working on the river up there. But I never spoke to him. Don't reckon he'd recognise me, but I did him.'

'Here we are,' Grace said. She took a photograph from the box her daughter found and handed it to Mary. 'I was going to give this to you later on. It's your mum and dad.'

Mary gasped in surprise. It was a wedding picture. The creased sepia photograph was of two smiling people, the woman holding flowers and wearing a plain but elegant dress, the man in a neat suit, against a painted background.

'I'm glad I never put it in one of those letters I sent you. I ask you, never giving you your letters!' Grace huffed. 'If I had known, Mary, I'd have been down there giving her a piece of my mind.'

<hr>

It was a pleasant spring evening as they crossed Waterloo Bridge. Mary stood for a moment, gazing along the Thames in a westerly direction, murmuring a prayer.

She was happy that she had found another picture of two people she barely remembered, but sad because she was worried about her brother. The police wanted to question him. She was unsure of just what that meant and how she would find him. He was two people, Lorna Denbie said. Was one of them a murderer?

She had a recurring dream, she told Archie. She was struggling underwater, trying to reach out to someone, but he was always just out of reach. Then someone held her and she felt safe again. She'd stopped having the dream many years ago. Then it started again the night she and Archie dived into the Thames to escape Black Bob and Davey Tupper a few months ago.

She'd never understood the dream until today.

AUTHOR'S NOTES

While the Victorian era is often associated with practical advancements in science and technology, interest in the paranormal, the supernatural and the occult was an attraction for many. The most popular forms included mesmerism, clairvoyance, crystal-gazing and, above all, spiritualism. The possibility of communicating with the souls of the departed fascinated many late Victorians, including Sir Arthur Conan Doyle, the creator of Sherlock Holmes.

The use of mediums was not an uncommon practice, nor was their use of fakery to convince others of their credibility. This could include trick photography, ventriloquism and other deceptions during a séance, which was made easier as these sessions were often conducted in darkness or semi-darkness.

The Irish Potato Famine, also known as the great

hunger, began in 1845 in Ireland. Tenant farmers relied heavily on the potato crop for food, and over the next seven years, a fungus-like infestation annually destroyed the crop with catastrophic results. Before it ended in 1852, the famine had caused roughly one million deaths from starvation and related problems, and forced another one million to leave their homeland as refugees. Many went to the United States.

Interest in Egypt, Egyptomania, began during the early years of the Napoleonic Wars when Napoleon launched an invasion of Egypt and Syria. By the Victorian era, Europe was seeing a proliferation of interest in Egyptian culture and design.

However, while scientific curiosity was undoubtedly involved, in some quarters, the interest became a spectacle and entertainment. Thomas Pettigrew, a surgeon, antiquary and author, would host private parties where he would unwrap and perform autopsies on mummies. Arthur Conan Doyle's short story, *Lot No. 249*, deals with the reanimation of a mummy.

Hatshepsut was the second confirmed female pharaoh in Egypt, reigning between 1473 and 1458 BC. During her reign, which was by and large peaceful, she constructed the great temple at Deir el-Bahari, Luxor, and launched successful sea voyages to the land of Punt, a place somewhere on the northeast coast of Africa.

After her death, her co-ruler and stepson/nephew, Thutmose III, would deface her monuments. In 2006,

Egyptologist Zahi Hawass located her mummy in the Cairo museum. She was identified from a tooth found in a box belonging to her that fitted the mummy exactly. It was concluded that she'd died in her fifties from an abscess following this tooth's extraction.

The British Museum, where Mary and Mrs Grady go, is in Bloomsbury, an area in central London, is a public institution dedicated to human history, art and culture. Established in 1753, and largely based on the collections of the scientist Sir Hans Sloane, it was open to the public in 1759, in Montagu House, on the site of the current building, as the first public national museum in the world. With a permanent collection of some eight million works, it is amongst the largest and most comprehensive in existence.

Finally, Occam's razor is a principle from philosophy. It states that if there are two explanations for an occurrence, then the one that requires the smallest number of assumptions is usually correct.

ACKNOWLEDGMENTS

A grateful thanks for all those who have helped in the writing of this book. And they are far too numerous to mention. So, for everyone who have encouraged me, for those who read the early drafts and pointed out my mistakes, and for the advice they have given me, my sincere thanks.

REVIEW REQUEST

If you have enjoyed reading this book, please leave a
review on Amazon, Goodreads or BookBub.
Every single review help new readers discover my books.

For more information you can visit my website:
https://saywackwrites.com

or contact me by email:
saywackwrites@gmail.com

or come and say Hi! on my facebook page:
https://www.facebook.com/SSSaywack

www.ingramcontent.com/pod-product-compliance
Lightning Source LLC
Chambersburg PA
CBHW061808190726
48289CB00007B/2115